CAÑON CREEK

OTHER FIVE STAR WESTERN TITLES BY LEWIS B. PATTEN:

Tincup in the Storm Country (1996)

Trail to Vicksburg (1997)

Death Rides the Denver Stage (1999)

The Woman at Ox-Yoke (2000)

Ride the Red Trail (2001)

Blood on the Grass (2002)

Guns of Vengeance (2003)

Back Trail (2004)

Sundown (2005)

Wild Waymire (2006)

Shadow of the Gun (2007)

Montana Gunfighter (2008)

Savage Desert (2009)

Gun This Man Down (2010)

Hang Him High (2011)

CAÑON CREEK

A WESTERN DUO

LEWIS B. PATTEN

FIVE STAR
A part of Gale, Cengage Learning

W

GALE
CENGAGE Learning®

Detroit • New York • San Francisco • New Haven, Conn • Waterville, Maine • London

GALE
CENGAGE Learning®

LIBRARY OF CONGRESS CATALOGING-IN-PUBLICATION DATA

Patten, Lewis B.
    Cañon Creek : a Western duo / by Lewis B. Patten. — 1st ed.
       p. cm.
    ISBN 978-1-4328-2608-6 (hardcover) — ISBN 1-4328-2608-5
(hardcover)
    I. Title.
PS3566.A79C36 2012
813'.54—dc23   2012016326

First Edition. First Printing: October 2012.
Published in conjunction with Golden West Literary Agency.
Find us on Facebook– https://www.facebook.com/FiveStarCengage
Visit our website– http://www.gale.cengage.com/fivestar/
Contact Five Star™ Publishing at FiveStar@cengage.com

Printed in Mexico
1 2 3 4 5 6 7 16 15 14 13 12

ADDITIONAL COPYRIGHT INFORMATION

CONTENTS

THE FEUD 9

CAÑON CREEK 147

★ ★ ★ ★ ★

THE FEUD

★ ★ ★ ★ ★

I

The five of them drew rein a quarter mile away, their sweated horses blowing from the run. In the moonlight, the white house before them loomed big and tall. The old one said harshly: "Clem, get the bunkhouse. Don't let anybody out."

"Yes, sir, Pa."

The old one said: "No shootin' if it can be helped. You got that ten-gauge double-barrel I told you to bring?"

"Yes, *sir*. It's loaded with buck."

The old one turned his head. "Nate, you an' Ross get the back door. Move quiet but move fast. Me an' Leon will take the front. You two get the downstairs, we'll get the up."

There were several grunts, indicating that Guy Dymond's instructions had been understood. "Let's go then," he said in his intemperate and angry voice.

He led down the wide lane toward the Majors house. While the five were still fifty yards away, two dogs ran out, barking and bristling. Guy heeled his horse and the animal broke into a gallop. The old man left the saddle in front of the wide front porch with its surrounding lilacs and honeysuckle and its climbing clematis. He headed for the door at a shambling run. One of the dogs came in with a rush and fastened his teeth in the old man's leg. With a growled curse, Guy brought his gun barrel down. The dog yelped once and then lay still.

Boots made a brief thunder on the wooden floor of the porch. Guy slammed the front door open and went in. Enough

11

moonlight came through the curtained windows for him to see. He beckoned to Leon, hearing the back door bang open as he did. He took the stairs two at a time and burst through the first bedroom door he reached.

Its occupant was Galt Majors, grizzled and white-haired, distinguished-looking even in the long white nightshirt that he wore. Guy said—"Keep him here, Leon."—and went on to the next bedroom, whose occupant turned out to be Donald Majors, Galt's oldest son.

Donald was just sitting up in bed as Guy shoved the shotgun muzzle into his stomach. "Where's Pres?" he demanded angrily.

"Next room." Donald was forty. He kept the ranch accounts and he sounded scared.

Guy said: "Get into your pa's room. Move, god damn you. Move!"

Barefooted, trembling, Donald got out of bed and hurried to the door. Guy waited long enough to see that he did as he was told. Then he went on to Preston Majors's room.

Pres was out of bed. He had his gun belt in his left hand and was drawing the gun from its holster with his right.

Guy said: "Don't!"

Preston looked at the shotgun in Guy Dymond's hands and froze. Guy said: "Drop it on the floor."

Gun and gun belt thudded to the floor. Guy said: "Get dressed. You're going with us."

Preston didn't ask why. He knew. He reached for his pants and Guy said angrily: "Your best. God damn you, put on your best."

Preston padded across the floor in his bare feet. He got a black suit out of the closet. He put on a white shirt, the suit pants, and a pair of black shoes. Guy had lit the lamp on the dresser. He went to the door now and shouted: "Nate?"

"Yes, sir?"

"Everything all right down there?"

"Yes, sir. We got James an' Robert."

Preston finished dressing. He was a big young man, nineteen years old, handsome, and a little spoiled. Guy gestured with the shotgun and Preston went out the door. In front of Galt Majors's room, Guy Dymond paused. Leon had lit a lamp. Galt Majors stood, spread-legged, in the middle of the room. His face was florid, his eyes filled with fury and outrage. Guy Dymond said: "Don't follow us, Galt. I got Pres. I'll kill him if you do."

"What's the meaning of this? Damn you, Dymond, I'll have the law on you."

"Do that, Galt. In the meantime, don't forget that we got Pres."

Galt Majors looked at Pres. "What's this all about?"

Pres couldn't meet his eyes. "I'll tell you later, Pa."

Guy Dymond jabbed the shotgun into his back. "Let's go. Come on, Leon."

Pres went down the stairs with Guy following. Leon followed Guy. At the foot of the stairs, Guy called: "Bring 'em in here, Nate!"

James Majors and his brother Robert came into the living room, followed by Nate and Ross, both of whom had guns. Guy said: "In case you two are tempted to follow, we're taking Pres."

Robert started to bluster. Guy said—"Shut up!"—and Robert Majors did. Guy herded Preston out the front door. His sons followed him. Guy gestured with the gun toward the extra horse they had brought along. "That one's yours. Get mounted and let's go."

Pres mounted meekly. Clem came from the bunkhouse, mounted his horse, and rode toward them. He seized the reins of Preston's horse. They thundered out of the yard and up the lane.

Pandemonium immediately broke out behind them. Men in underwear and nightshirts ran from the bunkhouse and began firing until a roar from the house halted them. Galt Majors and his sons had come out onto the porch.

Galt looked at the half-clad men. "They took Pres with them. Can anybody tell me why?"

Nobody spoke. Galt said: "Come on, come on."

Len Peabody, the foreman, said: "Pres has been seein' Lena Dymond. Maybe that's what it's all about."

Galt said: "That half-breed bitch?"

Nobody said anything. Galt said: "That's why the black suit. The son-of-a-bitch is going to make Pres marry her."

Still nobody said anything. Galt said: "Get dressed and get mounted up. We're going to stop it. I want everybody armed."

He turned and hurried back into the house, his sons following.

The Dymonds' six horses made a dull thunder in the ground as they raced toward Cottonwood Springs. Guy knew Galt Majors wasn't going to take this lying down. He had to be finished before Majors could intervene.

Cottonwood Springs was ten miles from the Majors Ranch. They reached it at 2:00 in the morning. There was a light in the parsonage. Guy hauled his lathered horse to a halt at the tie rail in front of the place. The others followed suit. They dismounted and tied.

Pres Majors remained on his horse. "I'm not going to do it. You can't force me to."

Guy was old, but he was big and he was strong. He grabbed Preston's leg and yanked him from the saddle. Pres hit the dirt on his back. The fall knocked all the air out of his lungs. Guy kicked him, hard, in the ribs, and Pres groaned and rolled away from him. Guy said: "Get up, you damn' whimperin' pup, and dust off your clothes."

Pres didn't get up immediately, so Guy kicked him again. After that Pres got painfully to his feet. He stood bent over, dragging air into his starving lungs. Guy said: "Dust off your clothes."

Feebly Preston dusted off his suit. Guy said: "In there. And don't say no to me again."

Meekly Preston headed for the door of the parsonage. Guy and his four sons followed close behind.

The preacher and his wife were waiting in the parlor. Lena Dymond was also there. She was a pretty, dark-skinned girl with high cheek bones and an expressive mouth. Her cheeks bore traces of tears.

She said: "Pa. . . ."

Guy Dymond said: "Shut up. You had your chance to talk. You could have said no to Pres six months ago."

She didn't speak again. Guy stared at the preacher, Wallace Good. "Get started, Preacher."

Good looked acutely uncomfortable. But he was plainly awed by Guy Dymond and his four big, unkempt sons. He nodded and glanced at Lena. "Shall we begin?"

Lena glanced up at Pres, her eyes trying to tell him she hadn't had anything to do with this. That shouldn't have been necessary. She was six months along and her baby was showing so that anyone could see. Pres came and stood beside her in front of the preacher, his face sullen, his eyes helplessly angry.

Good said—"Dearly beloved. . . ."—and paused, looking around at the angry faces, realizing what a travesty the words were. He went on stubbornly: ". . . we are gathered together in the sight of God and of this company to join this man and this woman in holy matrimony." He paused for breath.

Guy said harshly: "Get on with it, Preacher. We ain't got all night."

15

Good went on with the ceremony. His wife was very pale. The ceremony was brief, but it seemed longer than it really was. When the time came for Pres to put a ring on Lena's finger, Guy supplied the ring, one that had been worn by his wife before her death. Lena began to cry softly when she recognized it.

Pres put the ring on her finger with trembling hands. She did not raise her glance, nor did he. He looked steadily down at her hand.

The preacher said: "According to the power vested in me, I now pronounce you man and wife."

Guy gave the preacher a $5 gold piece. Pres looked at him defiantly. "Now what?"

Guy was about five feet ten, but he weighed two hundred and fifty pounds. He appeared to be grossly fat, but that was as deceptive as his face, which could wreathe itself in genial smiles while the eyes stayed hard and cold. He was fat, all right, but the muscles built by a lifetime of fighting and hard work were underneath. He crossed the room to Pres. He slapped Pres hard on the side of the face. A red mark instantly appeared. Softly Guy asked: "What does a bridegroom usually do on his wedding night?"

"Where? I mean, where are we goin' to go?"

Guy slapped him again. Lena flinched. Guy asked: "You have got to ask me that?"

"I can't. . . ." Pres stopped, his face suddenly turning pale.

"What can't you do?"

"Nothing. I didn't mean nothing."

"Uhn-uh, I want to know. What can't you do?"

Pres looked down at Lena. Her face was stricken, but anger was growing in her, too. Guy insisted: "What can't you do?"

Pres straightened defiantly. He shouted: "I can't take her home! That's what I was going to say. I can't take her home! Do

16

you hear that, you old son-of-a-bitch? I can't take her home!"

Guy's voice was like the hissing of a dynamite fuse. "Why can't you take her home? She's your wife. Legally. The preacher just married you."

"That don't matter. The old man ain't goin' to let no Dymonds in his house."

"She's not a Dymond any more. She's a Majors. Her name is Lena Majors. Missus Lena Majors. And she's carryin' a Majors brat."

"But she's Indian. She's a half-breed at least. The old man ain't goin' to let no half-breeds in *his* house."

Guy Dymond's face was white with fury. He swung a fist. It connected solidly with Pres Majors's mouth. Pres went staggering back across the room. He crashed against a table, overturning it. There was blood on his mouth when he raised his head.

The preacher said in a shocked voice: "Mister Dymond, please. Can't you . . . ?" He stopped. He had been about to say: "Can't you take this outside?" Instead he said: "A wedding should be a time for happiness."

Guy growled: "This one ain't." He glared at Pres and at Lena, then swung his glance to cover his sons. "Go on outside."

They filed out the door into the street. Guy looked at Pres and said: "There's a buggy tied outside. Use it. Take her home."

"I. . . ." Pres's voice died.

Guy said softly: "You take her home or she'll be a widow before the sun comes up." He swung around and went through the door.

He heard a thunder of hoofs down the long street as Galt Majors, his sons, and his crew came riding into town. His heavy features were grim, his eyes as hard and cold as those of a rattlesnake.

II

The moon hung low in the western sky and dawn was silhouetting the horizon in the east as Galt Majors and his party hauled their lathered horses to a stop in front of the Cottonwood Springs Methodist Church.

Guy Dymond stood his ground before the parsonage, his sons clustered behind him. Lena was in the buggy and Pres was standing beside it. From the doorway of the parsonage, Wallace Good and his wife peered out, white-faced and scared.

Guy Dymond said: "It's over. They're hitched."

Galt Majors glanced toward the parsonage. He could see Good and his wife standing there. He called: "Is that right, Preacher?"

Good's voice was faint and scared. "That's right, Mister Majors."

Majors looked at Guy. "Damn you to hell."

"She's better than Pres by one hell of a lot."

"A half-breed! That's what she is!"

"Go on home. Make the best of it."

"Be damned if I will!"

"You will. You ain't got no other choice."

"No other choice? Are you crazy? I don't have to take that half-Indian slut into *my* house."

Guy moved with startling swiftness for a man his size and age. One moment he was ten feet away from Galt. The next he was beside him, yanking him out of his saddle the same way he had with Pres. He kept the horse's bulk between himself and Galt's sons and crew so that they couldn't shoot.

With Galt on the ground, he straddled the man, his shotgun against the base of Galt Majors's skull. He roared: "Hold it! Hold it, or, by God, I'll blow his head off!"

Everybody froze right where they were. Guy Dymond said:

"Tell 'em to go home."

"Be damned if I will."

"You'll be damned all right. And you'll be dead. Tell 'em!" He jabbed the shotgun muzzle harder against the base of Galt Majors's skull. The man grunted with the pain. Lying there on the ground with the one man he hated most in all the world straddling him, he called: "Go on home, all of you! Do what I say."

Len Peabody asked: "What about you, Mister Majors?"

"I'll be all right! Now get the hell out of here!"

Guy jabbed the gun hard against the base of his skull once more. "Tell Pres to take his wife and go along with them."

"Be damned if I will!"

"You said that once before. I'm going to count to five." There was a deadly promise in Guy Dymond's voice and Galt knew he *would* shoot if he wasn't instantly obeyed. There was more to this than making an honest woman out of a pregnant girl. Galt Majors knew that better than anybody else.

He called in a voice that was thin with rage: "Pres?"

"Yes, Pa?"

"Take her home. I'll be along."

"Yes, sir, Pa." Pres climbed into the buggy and slapped the horse's back with the reins. The animal trotted down the street.

Len Peabody and the others hesitated a moment, uneasy and uncertain. Then Peabody said—"Come on. Do what he says."— and turned his horse. He touched spurs to the horse's sides and trotted after the buggy into the predawn gloom. The others followed him.

Guy raised his head and looked at his sons. "Go home. I'll be along."

Without protest, they got their horses, mounted, and rode away, leaving the two older men alone in the street. Guy looked toward the parsonage and lifted his voice to call: "Shut the door, Preacher. It's over now."

Good closed the door obediently. Galt said between clenched teeth: "Are you going to let me up?"

"I'll let you up. After I've said what I've got to say."

"Well, say it. Say it and get it over with."

"All right. I'll say it. I should have killed you twenty-five years ago. I don't know why I didn't. But your son ain't going to get away with what you did. You take Lena into your house. If you don't, I'm going to kill Pres and after that I'm going to kill you."

"That all?"

"Not quite." Guy withdrew the shotgun muzzle from Galt Majors's head. Dropping to his knees, he put his hand on the back of Majors's head and suddenly shoved his face down into the dirt. He said savagely: "Eat a little of that, you son-of-a-bitch! Find out what it tastes like!"

He got up, then, holding the shotgun ready. Majors struggled to his feet, spitting dirt out of his mouth. When he could talk, he said furiously: "I'll get even with you for this."

"Maybe. But whether you do or not, you learned one thing tonight. You can't use people forever without havin' to pay the bill. Neither you nor your spoiled rotten sons."

"I'm going to the law. I'll have you thrown in jail."

"Come on, by God. We'll both go. Let's just see what Sherm Gatewood has to say about all this."

Gatewood was the sheriff. He'd be sound asleep at this hour, but neither Guy Dymond nor Galt Majors cared about a thing like that.

Galt swung to his horse and galloped down the street. Guy, slower to mount, followed, also galloping. The sky was lighter now. Guy was grinning with long-deferred satisfaction. Galt Majors had been high-and-mightying it over the Dymond family for twenty-five years. Now, whether he liked it or not, he had a Dymond in his house. He actually had a Dymond in his house.

Gatewood had a small frame house next to the jail. Its windows were dark. By the time Guy arrived, Galt was pounding on the door with his fist. A sleepy voice came peevishly from inside. "All right! All right! Wait till I put on my pants."

Light flickered in the window and the door opened. Sherm Gatewood stood there clad in a long white nightshirt that had been tucked into his pants. He was barefooted. He said: "Lord, couldn't it wait until I got up?"

"Not this. No, sir," Galt Majors said angrily.

"All right. Come on in." Gatewood stood back from the door. He was a tall and strongly built man who looked to be about thirty. He wore a long, drooping mustache that completely hid his mouth. His face was lean and dark, with high cheek bones, but with Gatewood there was no question of Indian blood. His hair was as yellow as fresh-threshed straw.

Galt and Guy went in. Galt said furiously: "I want him arrested, Sherm. He and his sons came storming into my house a couple of hours ago, waving guns and threatening to kill everybody."

"What for?" Gatewood looked puzzled and confused.

"He kidnapped Pres, that's what for."

"Why would he want to kidnap Pres?"

"Claimed he'd got Lena in a family way. Hauled him in here to town at gunpoint an' forced the preacher to marry them."

Gatewood turned his head and stared skeptically at Guy. "Is that true?"

"It's true."

Galt said: "I want him arrested. I want him in jail."

"All right. What charges?"

"Kidnapping. Assault."

"Assault?"

"He yanked me off my horse. Shoved my face in the dirt."

21

"You want me to put that on the complaint?"

"Well, no. Just say assault."

"When it comes to trial, you'll have to say what he did. You'll have to say he made you eat dirt." There was a derisive sparkle in Gatewood's eyes.

"Dammit, Gatewood, don't you get smart with me."

"No, sir. What about the complaint?"

"Forget it."

"Yes, sir. Do you want me to forget the kidnapping complaint, too?"

"Forget the whole damn' thing!" Galt Majors glared helplessly at the sheriff and at Guy Dymond for a moment. Then he turned and left, slamming the door viciously behind him. The two heard the thunder of his horse's hoofs as he pounded down the street.

Gatewood coldly looked at Guy. "So you made Pres marry her?"

"He's the one that got her in trouble, ain't he?"

"I didn't know she was in trouble. I haven't seen her for months. Are you going to try and force Galt to keep her out at his house?"

"She's his daughter-in-law. He'd better keep her there or I'll make him wish he had."

"You're really getting even, aren't you? And using Lena to do it."

"Pres is the one that got her in a family way."

Gatewood's voice turned colder. "You want anything more from me?"

Guy Dymond shook his head.

"Then get the hell out of here and let me go back to bed."

Dymond scowled, but he went obediently out the door, slamming it but not as violently as Majors had.

Gatewood heard the pound of his horse going down the

street. He turned disgustedly and went into the tiny kitchen at the back of the house. He built up the fire in the stove and put some coffee on. He began to pace angrily back and forth.

There had been a time when he'd gone with Lena Dymond himself. Now he tried to remember what it was that had caused the quarrel over which they had broken up. He couldn't. It had to have been something pretty inconsequential, he thought, if he couldn't even remember what it had been. He'd been sorry for the breakup, though, and he was still sorry. He still thought a lot of Lena despite what her father said had happened since.

Furthermore, he thought he understood what had gotten her into her present predicament. Maybe the members of the Dymond family loved each other, but, if they did, they most certainly never let it show. And Lena, as starved for affection as a lost puppy, had been easy prey for Pres Majors, who had a lot of experience in making girls believe the lies he told. He had probably told her he'd marry her, but he had never intended to. He had used her the same way people said Galt Majors had used her Indian mother twenty-five years before.

That, of course, was what really lay behind the enmity between Guy Dymond and Galt Majors, Gatewood thought. The success of the Majors family and the troubles that had beset the Dymond family had only compounded the original enmity and made it worse. Galt Majors had thousands of acres of good grass. He cut ten thousand tons of hay off his bottom land.

Dymond's ranch, on the other hand, lay back in the hills where grass was scarce. He was lucky if he could cut fifty tons of hay to see his cattle through the winter. Wealth had given Galt Majors power and standing in the community. Poverty and mixed blood had made outcasts of the Dymond family.

The coffee boiled over and Gatewood poured himself a cup, after which he put the pot on the back of the stove. Whatever had caused the enmity between the two families, the happenings tonight would bring it to a boil. Gatewood had the uneasy feeling that more violence was coming, and he knew that each act of violence would bring on another, worse than the one that had preceded it.

He would be in the middle, charged with keeping the peace, with bringing to justice all violators of the law. He cursed sourly to himself. Guy Dymond thought he was pretty smart, forcing Lena on Galt Majors and shoving Majors's face into the dirt. But he wasn't smart. Galt Majors might be more civilized than Dymond was, but he was just as dangerous. Pushed too far, he would retaliate with equal violence.

Once more Gatewood thought of Lena and wished there was some way he could make this easier for her. But he knew that there was not. She was carrying Pres Majors's child, and that put her squarely in the middle of it.

She would suffer with the others, maybe even more because she was more sensitive than the men.

Hearing that she was carrying Pres Majors's child had been a brutal shock. Yet even while it hurt, it had not occurred to him to lay the blame on her.

Realizing this, he knew he still cared considerably for her. He cared what happened to her. He told himself bitterly that he should have cared more when they broke up. He could have made up with her if he'd tried. But he had been too proud. And now it was too late.

III

Galt Majors spurred his horse repeatedly as the animal thundered through the town. At top speed, he left Cottonwood Springs and headed toward home.

He couldn't recall ever having been more furious. He could still taste the grit of the street in his mouth and he could still taste the bitter gall of humiliation because it had been Guy Dymond who had put it there. Right now he could cheerfully have killed Guy. But he would not, because he would have to pay for it if he did. There were better ways of getting back at Guy.

The first way was, of course, through Lena. He couldn't change the fact that she was legally Preston's wife. But he didn't have to let her stay at the ranch. He didn't have to let Guy get away with forcing her on him.

His horse's neck was lathered and the animal was faltering. Galt reluctantly pulled him in. The horse stood in the middle of the road, breathing hard and trembling.

Galt realized that he was also trembling. He got down and led the horse along the road. Gradually, as he walked, his legs steadied. But his anger did not cool. Nor did his determination to get even with Guy Dymond fade. He walked for almost a mile, until the horse was rested and cooled, until his own fury had similarly cooled. Then he mounted again and continued toward home, holding the horse to a steady trot.

However hard he tried, he could not put the events of the past few hours out of his mind. Waking with the Dymonds thundering through the house still seemed like a nightmare to him, as did the kidnapping of Pres. The confrontation in town would make his face feel hot whenever he remembered it for a long, long time to come. But the ultimate, the crowning indignity had come when he was yanked from his horse and made to eat dirt in the street with his sons and the crew looking on.

He thought about Lena. She looked like her mother had twenty-five years ago. The resemblance was, in fact, startling. That was another reason he didn't want her around. He didn't want to remember what had happened twenty-five years ago. He had been young, foolish, and hot-blooded, or he wouldn't have been stupid enough to bed an Indian squaw, particularly when she was someone else's wife.

He'd paid for that. His face burned, remembering. Guy had caught him with her and had shot him. He'd damn near killed him, and would have except for the intervention of a man he'd had working for him.

No. He didn't want Lena around to remind him of those unpleasant happenings.

He reached the ranch and rode into the yard. Len Peabody was there, along with Galt's sons, Donald, James, and Robert. Peabody looked up at him. "You all right, boss?"

He nodded curtly. "I'm all right."

"You mad at us for leavin' the way we did?"

Majors shook his head. "No. I told you to."

"We figured if we tried to help, the son-of-a-bitch would do what he said he'd do."

Galt nodded shortly. "Where's Pres? And where's that girl?"

"In the house."

Galt looked at his three sons. "Find something to do. For Christ's sake, don't just stand around all day."

"Sure, Pa." All three answered simultaneously, as if they still were boys instead of men fully grown. They hurried away in the direction of the barn.

Galt gave his horse's reins to Peabody. He stalked toward the house, noting that the buggy in which Pres had brought Lena home still stood in front of it, a tether weight clipped to the horse's bridle. Good, he thought sourly. She could use it getting back to town.

He went into the house, slamming the door savagely behind him. He roared: "Pres!"

"Out here, Pa," came Pres's answering voice from the kitchen. Galt went to the kitchen door. Lena was standing beside the stove, her back to it. Pres was standing across the room, facing her. The faces of both were flushed and it was obvious that they had been arguing.

Galt stared icily at the girl. "Get out of here!"

Pres protested: "Pa, you can't. Maybe it ain't what you wanted, but we're married now. We owe her something. We. . . ."

Galt didn't even turn his head. He said: "Shut up!"

"But. . . ."

Galt now turned his head and fixed his stony eyes on Pres. "Damn you, I said shut up!"

The flush on Pres's face deepened. He shot a quick glance at Lena, then glanced back at his father again. He opened his mouth to speak, changed his mind, and closed it again.

Galt repeated coldly to the girl: "I said, get out of here."

She was only eighteen. She had been dominated by her father and brothers all her life and right now she was terrified. But she held her chin high and managed to keep all but a small tremor out of her voice: "I have every intention of leaving here."

"Then do it. Now."

Pres stepped forward. "Pa, damn it, she's my wife. You can't order her out of here like she was. . . ."

"Like she was what? A dirty Indian squaw?"

"Pa, stop it. Or. . . ."

"Or what, you snivelin' pup?"

"Or I'll keep her here." Pres started across the room toward Lena, perhaps to reassure her, perhaps only to stand beside her and face his father by her side. Galt came rushing into the room and swung a hand. The flat of it collided sharply with the side of Pres's face. Pres staggered to one side. Pure reflex made him raise his hands, clenched into fists, as if to defend himself.

At the sight of his son's clenched fists, something snapped in Galt. He set himself and swung one of his own fists with brutal efficiency. It slammed into Pres's jaw and sent him staggering back across the room. He slammed into the woodbox and fell into it, ending up on his back.

But Galt wasn't satisfied. He rushed to Pres, seized his shirt front, and yanked him up. He slammed a fist squarely into the middle of Pres's face, drew it back, and struck again

Lena screamed: "Stop it! Stop it!" She picked up a cast-iron skillet as if she would strike Galt with it. He dropped Pres and turned, threateningly.

Lena put the skillet down. She said: "I'm going."

"Then go, you Indian bitch!"

Lena fled. Pres was struggling to get to his feet. He yelled: "Wait!"

She didn't stop, but she heard Galt's roar: "What the hell do you mean, wait?"

"I'm going after her."

"The hell you are!"

Lena reached the front door. She went through it, running, and jumped down the three steps off the porch. She unclipped the tether weight, picked it up, and threw it into the buggy. The door of the Majors house slammed open and Pres came out. "Wait! I'm going with you." His mouth was smashed and bleeding. Blood ran from both nostrils and dripped onto the front of his shirt.

Galt came through the door ten feet behind Pres. Red-faced, glowering, he stood on the porch, glaring at Lena and at his son.

Lena shook her head. "No."

Pres said: "No? We're married. You ain't got no choice." Again she shook her head.

Galt said disgustedly: "Let her go, stupid. It's good riddance, if you ask me."

With a surprising amount of suddenly acquired backbone, Pres repeated stubbornly: "No, by God. We're married. That's my kid inside of her. If we can't stay here, we'll go some place else. But I'm stayin' with her no matter where she goes." He went to the buggy and put a hand on the horse's bridle, staring around defiantly at Galt.

Lena was close to tears but she was determined that Galt Majors wasn't going to see her cry. To Pres she said: "Let go, I don't want you. It's over."

He did not release the horse. She put a hand on the buggy whip but she did not yet remove it from its socket. Feeling the flood of tears scalding her eyes, she said: "Damn you, let go. Just because I made one mistake doesn't mean I'm going to keep on making them."

He repeated stubbornly. "I'm going with you."

She removed the whip. Raised half out of the seat, she flayed the horse's back with it. The animal jumped forward, but Pres hung on.

Terrified to be whipped and held at the same time, the horse reared. Still Pres hung on, by his weight dragging the horse down again. Lena, her face white, her eyes swimming now, deliberately laid the whip on Pres. It cut him across the face and one side of the neck, leaving an angry welt.

He released the horse and the animal sprang forward. The wheel struck him as it passed, knocking him sprawling into the dust. The buggy whirled away up the lane.

Lena was sobbing now openly. Tears so blurred her eyes that she could scarcely see. But she kept flaying the back of buggy horse, forcing him to an ever greater speed. The buggy careened from side to side, threatening each moment to overturn.

Pres stumbled to his feet. He stared into the cloud of dust raised by the buggy wheels. He knew he should go after her. He also knew that he would not. He didn't love her. He didn't want her any more than his father had wanted her mother twenty-five years ago. She was pretty and he had pursued her the same way he pursued every other girl that attracted him. But it couldn't last despite what he had said to his father a few moments before.

He stared for a moment at Galt. Then without a word he stalked into the house and climbed the stairs to his room, sulking the same way he had when he was a little boy. Galt was rich, and someday a fourth of all this would belong to him. In the meantime, he had everything he wanted, everything that money could buy.

But, throughout his growing years, he had paid a fearful price for everything money could buy. He had given up his manhood and now it was too late for him to get it back.

Not until she was a mile from the Majors Ranch house did Lena let the buggy horse slow to a walk. The animal was lathered and breathing hard.

Dabbing at her eyes with a handkerchief, Lena turned her head and looked behind, half expecting to see some kind of pursuit. There was none. The dust raised by the horse's hoofs and by the buggy wheels hung thinly in the air.

She had escaped from Pres and from the Majors Ranch, but she suddenly realized there was no escape from what her father had done to her by forcing the marriage at the point of a gun. By now it was all over town. Everybody knew.

And she was aware, furthermore, why he had done it. Not to make her condition respectable. Not to give the baby a name. Not even to uphold the honor of the family.

No. He had done it because Galt Majors had had an affair with her mother twenty-five years ago, before she was born. He had done it to get even with Galt for that.

She felt a sudden, overpowering bitterness. She hated her father, she told herself. She hated him.

And yet, in the back of her mind, she knew her troubles had not been caused by anything her father had done. She had caused this trouble by herself. She had said yes to Pres when she should have maintained a steady no.

Her life was over, she thought bleakly. No decent man would want her now. She was half Indian, and, if that wasn't enough, she had an illegitimate child.

She began to weep again. Miserable, she thought of Sherm Gatewood. She could not remember what they had quarreled about. Suddenly she straightened and dried her eyes. This wasn't the end of the world. She would have the child, and nobody could take it away from her.

And besides, crying never solved anything. She slapped the horse's back with the reins and the animal broke into a trot.

IV

Cottonwood Springs got its name from the natural springs that created a small lake a quarter of a league across in an area surrounded by cottonwood trees five miles west of town. It didn't really look like much of a lake, but that was the name it had provided the town.

Lena Dymond drove her buggy into town at midmorning, now holding the horse to a plodding walk.

At the edge of town, she realized suddenly that she had no place to go. She had no money of her own. She had been dependent throughout her life on her father. When she needed something, she asked him to buy it for her at Ledbetter's store. She had never had a dollar of her own.

She drove aimlessly up the street, trying to decide what she was going to do. Fear was a coldness along her spine. But equally compelling was her determination that she would not go back to her father's ranch.

Other people worked, she thought. Other people supported themselves. Then why couldn't she? The trouble was she didn't know where to start.

Passing the jail, she heard the door close and glanced toward the sound. She instantly glanced away again. Driving on, she heard Sherm Gatewood call: "Hey! Lena!"

She didn't stop. She didn't believe she could talk to the sheriff right now without bursting into tears. So much had happened in the last few hours and she'd had no sleep at all last night.

But she didn't have a choice. Gatewood caught up and seized the bridle of the buggy horse. "Whoa!" The horse stopped and Gatewood turned toward her. "I thought you were out at the Majors Ranch."

"What if I was?" There was a challenging edge to her voice.

He said soothingly: "Easy now. I didn't mean anything."

"Then suppose you let me go."

"Where are you going?"

"I don't believe that is any of your business, Mister Gatewood."

"*Mister* Gatewood?" He started to make a joking comment, stopped when he saw the expression on her face. In a more serious tone he asked: "What are you going to do, Lena? Are you going home?"

She shook her head. "That is the one thing I do not intend to do."

"What about Pres?"

She opened her mouth to reply, then closed it again. Her face flushed and her eyes sparkled. "You're asking a lot of nosy questions, Mister Gatewood."

He nodded. "I guess I was. I just thought maybe I could help."

"Thank you, I will not require any help. I can manage quite well all by myself."

"Then there's nothing I can do?"

"You can release my horse."

He nodded, released the horse's bridle, and stepped away. Lena felt like crying out to him. She felt like bursting into tears. She did neither. She slapped the back of the buggy horse with the reins and the animal plodded on up the street.

Sheriff Gatewood watched her go. He hadn't missed the dried sweat that still showed on the horse's neck, nor the way the wet hair was matted down beneath the harness straps. He had seen how close Lena was to tears.

He had wanted to reach up, lift her down, and take her in his arms. But he'd known that was impossible. Anything he did for her would be misinterpreted. She would think it was pity. Everybody else would think it was because he, instead of Pres, was the father of her child.

He watched the buggy go on down the street, frowning. *Where the hell is she going to go?* he asked himself. *What is she going to do?* There weren't any jobs in Cottonwood Springs for a girl, particularly one as far along as Lena was. She wouldn't be able to do any heavy work. In a month or two she probably wouldn't be able to work at all.

The buggy turned the corner two blocks up the street and disappeared. With an angry curse, Gatewood went back into the jail.

Preston Majors took the stairs two at a time. He went into his room and slammed the door. He walked to the window and stared at the buggy, now little more than a dot on the road leading to Cottonwood Springs.

The last eight hours had been a nightmare, beginning with Guy Dymond bursting in and forcing him to go with him into town where the shotgun marriage had then taken place.

That was bad enough. But the humiliation his father had heaped on him in front of Lena. . . . His face burned as he thought of it. And as if that wasn't enough, Lena had made it amply clear what she thought of him when she refused to let him accompany her to town, when she had laid the buggy whip on him to make him let go of the horse.

He heard his father come into the house. He heard him moving about and shortly thereafter heard him leave again. Looking out the window, he saw his father cross the yard to the corral. Galt caught and saddled a horse, mounted, and rode away, heading into the bed of Coyote Creek, which meandered through the ranch. He did not reappear.

Pres began to pace nervously back and forth. *Damn Guy Dymond,* he thought. *And damn his father!* Neither of them had the right to humiliate him the way they had.

He longed to do something that would, in some way, restore his pride. But what could he do? Everybody must know, by now, about the forced marriage that had taken place in the early morning hours in Cottonwood Springs. Before long everybody would know that Galt had refused to let Lena stay at the Majors Ranch. They would know that Pres had meekly permitted Lena to be driven away. He realized suddenly that if he let things stay as they were now, he wouldn't dare show his face in town. He'd be laughed at in the saloons. No girl would have anything to do with him.

Having decided that, he crammed his hat on his head and went downstairs. He crossed the yard to the corral and caught a horse. One of his brothers yelled at him from the barn, but he did not reply. He mounted and spurred the horse. He galloped up the lane toward town. Maybe he could still catch Lena, he thought, before she got to town. If not, he'd reach town at almost the same time she did.

But what was he going to do when he did face Lena again? What if she still wouldn't have anything to do with him?

Hell, at least everybody would know he'd tried, he told himself. They'd know he hadn't let his father run her off without protesting it. He wouldn't be an outcast in town. Shotgun marriages weren't exactly new and it wasn't unusual for a girl to refuse to live with her new husband. Even if Lena wouldn't have anything more to do with him, he would have behaved in an acceptable way. Nobody could blame him after that.

He held the horse to a steady gallop all the way to town. He did not see Lena on the road, nor did he see her when he entered town.

Passing the jail, though, he heard Gatewood yell: "Pres! I want to talk to you!"

He drew the horse to a halt. Gatewood came into the street and looked up at him. "What the hell happened out there at your place?"

"I don't know what business it is of yours."

Gatewood's eyes gleamed. "I'm making it my business. Answer my question."

"Pa ran her off. I tried to go with her but she took a cut at me with the buggy whip."

"Well, she needs help. You'd better find her and at least see that she has some money and a place to stay."

"Don't tell me what to do."

Gatewood said: "Damn it, I *am* telling you."

Pres blurted: "Maybe it wasn't me at all. Maybe, by God, it was you."

Something flared in Gatewood's mind and he took no time to consider the foolishness of it. He made a leap at Pres, seized his arm, and yanked him out of his saddle. The startled horse spooked away, trotted up the street for fifty feet, and stopped.

Pres hit the ground with a thump. Gatewood hauled him to his feet, both hands grasping the front of Pres's shirt. "What?" he roared.

"I . . . said . . . maybe it . . . was you."

Gatewood let go of him and swung a hard and bony fist. It landed squarely in the middle of Pres's face. His nose seemed almost to burst. He staggered back and sat down in the middle of the street, tears streaming from his eyes, blood streaming from his nose.

And suddenly all the indignity Pres had suffered in the last eight hours became a burden too heavy to be borne. He pushed himself to his feet. With an inarticulate sound of pure fury, he rushed at Gatewood, head down like a bull. Gatewood met him, swinging, but Pres's force was too much. His head struck Gatewood fully in the chest and drove a monstrous grunt from him. Gatewood sat down this time, and Pres stood over him, panting as if he'd run for half a mile.

Sanity returned slowly to Gatewood's mind. This wasn't helping anyone, he realized, least of all Lena, who was the one that needed help. This would only stimulate the gossipmongers; this would only make things worse.

He struggled to his feet. Pres braced himself for an attack. Gatewood said wearily: "It's all right, Pres. Go on home."

"I've got to find her. I've got to see her."

Gatewood shrugged. "All right. See her then." He turned and went back into the jail.

Pres stared after him for several moments, puzzled. Then he turned, walked to his horse, and mounted him. He rode up the street, turned the next corner, and disappeared.

Gatewood stared out the window of the jail. Perhaps a dozen people had stopped to watch the fight. Now they formed several clusters, talking excitedly.

He had been a fool. He had let his temper get away from him. He had hurt Lena when all he wanted to do was help.

He began to pace nervously back and forth, deeply worried not only about Lena but also about what was happening. Animosity between Galt Majors and Guy Dymond had smoldered harmlessly for many years. Now it was out in the open. Guy had committed violence against Galt and against Galt's son. If Gatewood knew Galt, it would not go unpunished for very long.

Pres rode past, heading out of town again. Gatewood stepped out into the street. Pres turned his head warily.

"Find her?" Gatewood asked.

Pres nodded, scowling.

Gatewood could see Pres hadn't made any headway. He asked: "Where is she?"

"Up at the hotel. Sitting on the porch."

Gatewood watched Pres ride down the street. Then he turned and headed for the hotel. Lena had probably asked at the hotel for a job. If she was sitting on the porch, it meant she had been refused. She was probably sitting there, wondering what she was going to do next.

He turned the corner. He could see her buggy tied in front of the hotel. He could see her sitting on one of the rockers on the hotel porch. She looked small, sitting there. Small and helpless and alone, wearing her best dress with a light coat over it to help conceal her pregnancy.

Gatewood climbed the three steps to the hotel porch. She glanced up at him. Tears stood out in her eyes. Her cheeks were wet. She put up her hands and wiped them away, afterward looking up at him defiantly.

He put out his hand. "Come on."

"Come on where?"

"Never mind. Just come on."

She looked to right and left as if for an alternative. Then, resignedly, she took his hand and got to her feet. "Where are we going?"

He did not reply. Holding firmly to her hand so that she couldn't change her mind, he led her back along the street in the direction he had come.

At the door of his own small house he stopped. He said: "You stay here until you find something else."

"I can't. . . . I won't. . . ."

"You can and you will. I'll sleep next door at the jail. If you want to pay me for the house, you can cook my meals."

She did not look at him, but he could see her shoulders trembling. He opened the door and pushed her inside. He said: "I'll take the buggy down to the livery barn. Guy can get it there."

She turned and looked at him, her eyes filling again with tears. He said—"Never mind."—and firmly closed the door.

V

Gatewood walked back along the street to the hotel. He untied the buggy horse and climbed into the buggy. He drove the rig to the livery stable and up the plank ramp from the street, climbing down as Buck Thornburg, the liveryman, limped from his office.

Gatewood said: "This belongs to Guy Dymond. He'll be coming after it."

Buck took the horse's reins from him. "When?"

"I don't know. Probably today."

"He'll have to pay for a whole day. I can. . . ."

Gatewood said: "Charge him whatever you please. That's between you and him."

Buck led the horse away, the buggy wheels creaking as they rolled over the plank floor. Rig and horse disappeared out the back door. Gatewood waited, frowning slightly. When Buck returned, he asked: "You've been here a long time, haven't you?"

Buck nodded. "A long time." He was an old man, perhaps seventy. His right foot was twisted and misshapen, his right leg slightly shorter than the other one, causing him to limp. He shaved once a week, on Saturday night, so he usually had a growth of whiskers on his face. He chewed tobacco, and now he spat on the floor.

"What do you know about the trouble between Guy and Galt?"

"All there is, I reckon."

"Mind telling me? It looks like the damned thing is going to blow up and it might help if I knew what it was all about."

"Ain't a hell of a lot to tell. Started back in 'Sixty-Five as I recall. This town weren't much more'n a stage station, a store, an' a saloon. Galt had him a sod house out there where that big fancy house is now. Had two of them boys and his missus was showin' the third. Talk was she told him she weren't goin' to have no more. Havin' the second damn' near kilt her, she said. She was a woman to talk an' that's how everybody knew. Told Galt to find him another woman when the need got too strong. Well, he did. Found quite a few of 'em."

"Among them Guy Dymond's wife?"

"Yep. Guy got here a couple years after Galt did. Galt was claimin' all of the land along Coyote Creek, so Guy settled back in the hills. Didn't know hay was necessary for the hard winters here. Hadn't been here long enough to know. Well, Guy had him an Injun wife. Arapaho, they said. Didn't speak no English hardly, just a couple words here an' there. Pretty, though. Looked a lot like Lena does."

Gatewood waited. Buck rolled his tobacco cud around in his cheek and spat again. "Wasn't much of a town, Cottonwood Springs wasn't, but there was people. People on ranches an' a few in town. Back in 'Sixty-Five, there was still hostiles around. Injun troubles wasn't over with, not by one hell of a lot. So you can't hardly blame people for not exactly takin' to Guy's Injun squaw. He'd bring her to town an' the ladies wouldn't speak. Wouldn't even look at her. Or at him, when she was along. Pretty soon, Guy didn't bring her to town no more. Or take her any place. But he'd go. He got to goin' more an' more. What with the cattle work an' all, he was gone pretty near all the time."

"And Galt got to seeing her?"

Buck shrugged his thin shoulders. "I guess. Nobody knew what was goin' on. Nobody knew how Galt happened to start seein' her, or how long it had been goin' on. First anybody knew, they hauled Galt into town flat on his back in a wagon bed with a bullet in his gut. I seen the wagon an' it looked like there was a bucket of blood in the back of it."

"What happened then?"

"The storekeeper's wife, Miz Ledbetter, put him in bed over at her house. Wasn't no doctor for three hundred miles. She got the bullet out an' she watched over him. Nip an' tuck it was for a couple of weeks. But then old Galt, he began to mend."

"And Guy?"

"Well, we didn't have no jail, so the sheriff didn't arrest him then. Didn't know what the charge was goin' to be anyway. Not until they saw whether Galt was goin' to live or die."

"And then they arrested Guy?"

"When the circuit judge came through. They had a trial in the saloon. Had a hell of a time gettin' a jury. Took near every able-bodied man in the country."

"Including you?"

"Including me."

"How long did the trial take?"

"It was over the same day it started. They put the squaw on the stand but she didn't know much English, so they didn't get much out of her. Wasn't no lawyers, just the judge. Guy got up an' said he came home an' found Galt in bed with her. Said he shot him just like he'd shoot a skunk in the chicken house. Said he'd shoot him again, or any other man he found like that."

"They send him to jail?"

"Hell no. Turned him loose. Those days, you mess with a

man's wife, you was just askin' to be shot. Galt was lucky he wasn't kilt."

"What happened after that?"

"Well, Galt finally got well." Buck chuckled humorlessly. "Can't say I recollect him ever chasin' a skirt after that. An' nobody ever saw that Injun woman of Guy's again. She kept to home, never even goin' out of the house, the way I hear tell, though I suppose that ain't likely. Anyhow, nobody ever saw her afterward. She bore Guy them boys, an' Lena, so I reckon Guy stayed to home more'n he had been. Truth is, nobody ever knowed when she died. There wasn't no preacher or funeral. I reckon they just made up a box for her an' planted her all by theirselves."

"And Guy and Galt hated each other ever since?"

"Uhn-huh. Galt hated Guy for shootin' him, an' Guy hated Galt because everything he touched turned to gold whilst Guy was scratchin' out a bare livin' up there in the hills."

Gatewood said: "Thanks, Buck."

"Sure. Any time."

Gatewood went out and headed back toward the jail. It was getting close to noon.

Maybe, he thought, the trouble would stop. Maybe, having evicted Lena from his house, Galt would be willing to forget that Guy had shoved his face into the dirt. And maybe, having had the satisfaction of humbling his enemy, Guy would be willing to overlook the fact that Lena had been forced to leave the Majors Ranch.

He could only hope they would. Lena had suffered enough. The people in Cottonwood Springs weren't going to let her forget, but maybe if she stopped being the focal point of her father's and Galt's animosity, it would help.

Gatewood reached the jail. He glanced toward his house, but he didn't see any movement in the windows or outside in the yard. A plume of smoke rose from the tin chimney, so he knew Lena was still there.

He went into the jail. He sat down in his swivel chair and put his feet up on the desk. He packed his pipe and lit it.

He couldn't get rid of his uneasiness. The trouble *wasn't* over with. He knew it in his bones. Galt wasn't going to overlook having been made to eat dirt in front of his sons and crew. Guy wasn't going to overlook Lena's having been forced to leave the Majors Ranch.

A new and disturbing thought suddenly occurred to him. Lena's position as Pres's wife gave her an interest in the Majors Ranch. At least it would give her an interest if something should happen to Galt.

He wondered if that possibility had occurred to Guy. He wondered if Guy's insistence on the forced marriage hadn't been only the opening move of such a carefully thought-out plan.

It was ridiculous, he told himself. Guy wasn't a cold-blooded murderer. But however he tried, he couldn't put the thought out of his mind. Galt's death and Pres's would give Guy, through Lena, a one-quarter interest in the Majors Ranch, worth $100,000 at the very least.

That would be a tempting prize for anyone. And for Guy Dymond, who had been trying to scratch out a living on that bare-hill ranch for more than twenty-five years, it must be doubly tempting. Maybe too tempting to resist.

For a time, Galt Majors rode aimlessly along the bed of Coyote Creek. Usually when he was upset or worried, he rode out away from the house alone. It gave him a warm feeling to think that he could ride all day in the same direction and still not leave his own land. Usually riding this way calmed his thoughts. Today it did not.

He came on a bunch of forty or fifty cattle. They were fat and sleek. It made a difference when they came through the winter in good flesh, he thought. That was why the Majors Ranch was so much better than any of the others hereabouts. He had ten thousand head of cattle. He stacked a ton of hay for every one of them.

He could understand Guy's being envious. And now a sudden, disquieting thought occurred to him. What if there was more behind the shotgun marriage than simply making an honest woman out of Lena and giving her child a name? What if it was the opening move in a play to get control of part of the Majors Ranch?

Guy wouldn't dare, he thought. Or would he? Lena was married to Pres. If anything happened to him, a fourth interest in the ranch would go to Pres. And if anything happened to Pres, Lena would own that fourth.

The plan, of course, would only work if he and Pres were eliminated. He asked himself if Guy Dymond was capable of murdering them.

He decided that Guy was capable of any kind of violence— hot-blooded violence at least. He himself had been the victim of Guy's violence twenty-five years ago. He had nearly died. No, he wouldn't underestimate Guy.

How, then, would Guy react when he discovered that Lena had been forced to leave? Galt didn't hesitate about the answer to that. Guy would come storming out here, trying to force the Majors family to take her back. He'd force her on them by whatever means it took. After going to all the trouble of kidnapping Pres and forcing the marriage, he wasn't likely to permit her to be sent away. Not without a fight.

Galt asked himself how he would face that threat when it came. Was it worth an all-out fight with the Dymond family? Was it worth people getting killed?

He shook his head slowly. What seemed to be involved, Lena's presence at the Majors Ranch, wasn't worth an all-out fight. And yet he knew with a sudden, uneasy certainty that he didn't dare let Lena be installed out here as a permanent member of the family. Doing so would only make possible the success of Guy Dymond's plan. If, indeed, he had such a plan.

The sun was now high in the sky. It was almost noon, Galt thought. So much had happened in the last twelve hours. It seemed like a week ago that Guy and his sons had come storming into the house to kidnap Pres.

He turned his horse and headed back toward the ranch. Dinner would be on the table soon. It did not occur to him that he could eat no matter what time he got back. Habit was too strong. Dinner was at noon. That was when everybody ate.

Riding now at a steady trot, he thought of Pres and of his other sons. They'd be damned little good in a fight, he knew, and suddenly he wondered why.

He had probably ruined them, raising them, he thought bleakly. He had given them too much of a material nature and had demanded too little from them in the way of work and responsibility. Galt knew, perhaps better than anyone, that men are fired in the crucible of adversity. He'd carved this ranch out of Indian country, in the process fighting for his life half a dozen times. But his sons didn't know the meaning of adversity. Nor did they know what true independence was. He'd never let them be independent. He'd never let any one of them make a decision on his own. He had given them a lot, but he had exacted a fearful price.

He rode into the yard and put his horse into the corral. He hung up his saddle, then crossed the yard to the pump. Len Peabody was there, washing along with a couple of the hands. Galt said: "Guy might be coming back. Put a couple of men on guard. And keep enough men around here to defend the place."

"Yes, sir."

"Pres still in the house?"

"No, sir. He rode out just after you did."

"Where to?"

"He headed toward town. Goin' pretty fast. I figured he was tryin' to catch that girl."

Galt nodded and headed for the house. He was mildly surprised at Pres, but he discovered he was not displeased. Maybe Pres had some backbone after all.

VI

There was, in Guy Dymond, a warm feeling of satisfaction as he led his sons back toward the Dymond Ranch in the hills. He grinned slightly as he remembered how Galt had looked, spitting out the dirt he had been forced to eat. Maybe that would teach the uppity son-of-a-bitch a thing or two, thought Guy. Maybe that would teach him that he and his sons couldn't go around riding rough-shod over everyone. The bastards seemed to think they could have any woman, married or single, young or old, whenever they felt like it.

Well, he'd shown Galt twice now that the Dymond women were to be let alone. He'd shot Galt and nearly killed him twenty-five years ago for sneaking around with his wife behind his back. Today he'd forced Pres to marry Lena and make an honest woman out of her. He grinned more widely as, in his mind, he went over all the humiliations he had heaped on Galt and his family in the process of doing it. Not once did he give any consideration to how Lena might have felt.

Halfway home, however, it occurred to him that Galt might not allow Lena to stay at the Majors Ranch. Nothing was to prevent him from sending her back to town. And if Galt was allowed to get away with that, all his own sense of triumph would disappear.

He turned his head and looked at Ross. "Go on back to town. Stay there, and, if Lena shows up, you come out and let me know."

Ross nodded, his eyes brightening. "Sure, Pa." He hesitated and Guy asked shortly: "Well, what are you waitin' for?"

"Pa, could I have fifty cents? I might have to be in town all day."

Guy hesitated. Then, reluctantly, he took a half dollar from the pouch in his pocket and gave it to his son. Grinning, Ross thanked him and whirled his horse toward town. He galloped away, raising a cloud of dust. Guy and his remaining sons continued toward home.

Ross rode at a gallop for about half a mile. Then he pulled the horse into a walk. This way, he continued toward town, occasionally licking his dry lips as he thought how good a cold beer was going to taste when he arrived.

It had surprised him when his father gave him the money without even bellyaching about it. He'd asked for 50 cents in the hope of getting 25 cents. Two bits would have bought five beers. It still would, and he'd have the other two bits for another time. He could eat the free lunch in the saloon and wouldn't have to buy any food.

The saloon wasn't open when he arrived. Ernie Mead was sweeping the walk in front. Finished, he got a scoop shovel and began to scatter the horse droppings that had accumulated in front of the tie rail.

Ross dismounted and tied. He sat down on the bench in front of the saloon and rolled himself a cigarette. "What time you open up?"

Ernie shrugged. "When Dutch gets here."

"When's that?"

"Any time from now on, I guess. What you doin' in town this time of day?"

"Pa sent me." Ross did not elaborate.

"What was all the commotion around daybreak? You got any idea?"

"Why there was a weddin'. My sis an' Pres Majors."

"Lena? Married to Pres?" There was open incredulity in Ernie's voice.

"Why not?" Ross asked belligerently. "What's wrong with that?"

Ernie said hastily: "Nothin'. I didn't mean nothin' was wrong with it. It's only that you an' the Majors clan ain't never had too much use for each other."

"I suppose we ain't."

Ross was slightly mollified.

"How'd it happen?" Ernie asked.

Ross thought: *Hell, the whole town is goin' to know it soon enough.* He said: "Lena's in a family way."

"Pres, huh?"

"Uhn-huh. Pres."

"Where are they now?"

"Out at the Majors Ranch."

Ernie whistled. "Out at the Majors Ranch? Does old Galt know?"

"He knows."

"And he ain't done nothin'? He ain't run 'em off?"

"Not yet he ain't. Pa sent me to town so's I could let him know if Galt did run 'em off."

"What do you reckon your pa will do if he does?"

Ross shrugged. He didn't know. He didn't see what his father could do. You couldn't force somebody to keep somebody else at his ranch if he didn't want to.

Ernie said: "If he tries to force old Galt to keep her out there, there'll be a fight."

Ross nodded. He supposed there would be a fight. He

47

wondered if his father had considered the possibility.

Ernie said: "All legal, huh? By the preacher and everything?"

"Why sure. How else can people get married, anyway?"

Ernie chuckled.

Ross asked: "What's so damn' funny?"

Ernie was grinning. He was an old man, past seventy. He was stooped and weathered and wrinkled and he had only three teeth in front. He said: "If Lena's married to Pres, then she's kind of got an interest in the Majors Ranch, ain't she?"

"Not unless the old man dies."

Ernie said: "That's what I mean. If there was to be a fight and if old Galt was to get hisself killed, then Lena an' Pres would own a fourth of the Majors spread. An' if somethin' was to happen to Pres. . . ." He left the sentence dangling.

Ross frowned. He hadn't thought of that. But the old man was right. Lena's marriage to Pres did give her some rights.

Ernie took his broom and shovel into the saloon. After a few minutes he came to the door. "Hell, come on in. I guess I can draw you a beer. Dutch won't care."

Ross went in. He stood at the bar and Ernie drew him a beer. Ross pushed the half dollar toward him. Ernie said: "Let Dutch make the change."

Ross nodded. The beer wasn't as cold as it might have been, but it tasted good. He finished it and wiped his mouth with the back of his hand. He didn't even notice immediately when Ernie refilled it and pushed it along the bar to him. He was engrossed with thoughts of what a fourth interest in the huge Majors Ranch was worth.

They had ten thousand cattle. At $30 a head, that was $300,000. To say nothing of the land. And the house. And the money in the bank.

It was so unbelievable it staggered him, and he asked Ernie for a pencil and paper. Then, laboriously, he put down ten thousand and multiplied it by $30. The answer came out $300,000. If the ranch was worth as much more, then a fourth interest was worth the staggering sum of $150,000.

He put down $150,000 and divided it by six. The result was $25,000. That sum staggered him, too, but that was what each of them would get if the $150,000 was divided equally. It wouldn't be, of course, but whatever his share was, it would be a fortune. He could buy a ranch of his own some place. He could stock it and still have money left. He looked at the half dollar on the bar. He wouldn't have to ask Pa for money any more like a snot-nosed kid.

Ernie asked: "What you writin'?"

Ross crumpled the paper guiltily. He threw it into the spittoon. He picked up the second beer and gulped it down.

Ernie persisted: "What was you writin', Ross?"

"Nothin'. Just doin' a little figgerin'."

He picked up the 50 cents. "I got to go look around. I'll be back."

Ernie nodded. He didn't say anything about getting paid for the beer. But when Ross had gone, he fished the paper out of the spittoon. Luckily he had already cleaned them, so the paper was dry. He spread it out on the bar and looked at it.

It wasn't hard to figure out what it was, particularly remembering what they had been talking about. The ten thousand had to be the number of cattle Galt Majors had. The $30 must represent what Ross figured each of them was worth. He frowned a little over the $150,000, decided finally it was Ross's estimate of what a fourth interest in the entire Majors Ranch was worth. Dividing by six gave the share of each member of the Dymond family, provided it was divided among them equally.

It occurred to him that Sheriff Gatewood ought to have this paper. He ought to know what was going on in Ross Dymond's head.

He folded the paper carefully and put it into his pocket. Dutch came through the doors. He said: " 'Mornin', Ernie."

" 'Mornin', boss."

"Wasn't that Ross Dymond I saw leaving here?"

Ernie nodded. "He was waitin' for us to open up."

Dutch didn't mention the empty beer glass on the bar.

He took off his hat and coat and put his white apron on. Ernie went toward the door. "See you this afternoon."

"All right, Ernie."

Ernie went to the jail and opened the door. Gatewood glanced up from his desk. Ernie fished the folded paper from his pocket. "Don't like tellin' tales but I thought this was somethin' you ought to know."

"What, Ernie?"

"This paper. It was wrote by Ross Dymond down in the saloon a little while ago. We was talkin' about Lena bein' part of the Majors family now an' havin' some interest in the place. We talked some about what the Majors place was worth."

Gatewood looked at the paper. His face showed no change of expression. He said: "Thanks, Ernie."

"You think . . . ?"

Gatewood shook his head. "No law against wanting what your neighbor's got. It's taking it that's against the law."

"You think I shouldn't have come here with this?"

"I don't think that at all. If I know what's going on in Ross Dymond's head, maybe I can keep anything from happening."

Ernie nodded and went out. Gatewood had reassured him, but he still wished he'd left the paper in the spittoon. He felt like a meddling old fool.

Ross found the buggy out back of the livery stable. He found out from Buck Thornton that Lena had gone to the sheriff's little house. When he reached the house, he didn't knock on the door, but sat down on the front steps.

After ten minutes or so, Lena came out. She had seen him sitting out there. Ross said: "Hello, Sis."

She looked at him without warmth. "What do you want?"

"Pa sent me."

"To watch for me? In case I left the Majors place and came to town?"

He nodded.

"Well, you can go and tell him that I'm in town. Tell him I'm not going back to the Majors Ranch and that I'm not coming home."

He nodded. "I'll tell him, but you know Pa. He figures you got rights out at the Majors Ranch. He aims to see you don't give 'em up."

"If I do have rights, they're mine. They don't belong to Pa."

"You ain't of age. What's yours belongs to Pa."

She looked at him angrily. "Is that all you came to say? If it is, you can go back home and report to him."

"It's all. But if I was you, I'd skedaddle back to the Majors place."

"I couldn't even if I wanted to. I was told to leave."

"By Galt?"

"By Galt."

"And Pres didn't do anything?"

"Pres is like you and me and Clem and Nate and Leon. He does what he's told to do. Only I'm through doing what anybody tells me to. You can tell Pa that, too, if you want."

"I'll tell him. But he ain't goin' to like it. He'll probably come into town an' whop the hell out of you. An' then take you back to the Majors place."

"He hadn't better try."

Ross grinned. "What would you do?"

"I'd . . . I don't know. But I'd do something."

"Don't you *want* to live out there? In that big fancy house?"

"No, I don't. And Pa doesn't want me to live out there, either. He's just using me as a weapon against Galt Majors."

Ross said: "When old Galt dies, you an' Pres will own a fourth of the whole damn' place."

"And Pa and you and the others will try getting your hands on it. Is that what you mean?"

"Maybe. What's so wrong with that? We been clawin' for a livin' all our lives. What's wrong with wantin' somethin' more?"

"Nothing, as long as you earn it for yourself."

He could see nothing was to be gained by talking any more to her. He walked back toward the saloon, where his horse still was tied. He intended to spend at least half of the 50 cents before going home. Guy might want him to give back what change was left.

Lena looked bleakly after him. She had been turned down in the hotel when she asked them for a job. She didn't know what she was going to do. But she wasn't going home. And she wasn't going back to the Majors Ranch, or back to Pres. Of that much she was very sure. She didn't really want to stay in Sherm Gatewood's house, but she realized that she had nowhere else to go. She went back inside.

VII

Ross spent the entire 50 cents at the saloon, drinking beer. He ate from the free lunch at the end of the bar. It was mid-afternoon before he started home.

He staggered as he crossed the walk to untie his horse. He mounted, hitting the saddle heavily. He was grinning foolishly and he felt very good. He sank spurs suddenly into his horse's sides, gave a wild yell, and galloped out of town.

It was nearly suppertime when he reached home. He halted his horse where the narrow, two-track road came over a barren ridge, and stared at the scattered collection of buildings down below.

Some of them were built out of creosoted railroad ties, chinked with clay. Others were built of poles. Still others were of frame construction. Guy built with whatever material was available. He had stolen the ties from the railroad thirty miles away. He had torn down abandoned buildings wherever he found them for the other material. He had even torn down corrals and shipping pens.

Roofs were shingled with tin cans that had been flattened. Now they were a uniform rusty red. A dog barked, and another. Ross touched his horse's sides with his spurs and trotted down the slope.

Guy came out of the house and stood there, staring toward him. The sun had slid well down the western sky and now cast long shadows on the ground. Ross halted in front of Guy. "She's in town, all right. Says Galt Majors told her to leave."

Guy scowled angrily. "Well, by God, we'll see about that."

"She says she ain't goin' back. Says she ain't comin' back here, neither."

"She'll do what I tell her to."

"She says you can't make her go back to Galt's."

Guy said: "Go do your chores." He glared up at Ross a moment, then added disgustedly: "You're drunk."

"No I ain't. I just had a couple of beers."

"A couple? How much you got left out of that fifty cents?"

"I ain't got anything. I had to eat."

Guy snorted. "Eat, hell. You wouldn't pay for food when you could eat the free lunch in the saloon. You must've had ten beers."

Ross grinned foolishly. His father did not return the grin. He repeated harshly: "Do your chores. After supper we're all goin' to town."

"What you goin' to do?"

"I'm goin'to teach that uppity bunch that Lena's part of their family now."

"How you goin' to do that?"

"Never mind. Just get your chores done. And then stick your head under the pump. I should've known better than to give you fifty cents all at once."

Ross turned his horse and rode away toward the corral. Guy stood looking after him.

He had been savoring his triumph over Galt Majors all day, but now the edge of it had dulled. Ross's news had caused a letdown in the way he felt. Damn Galt Majors anyhow. He wasn't going to get away with running Lena off. She was part of his family now. She was legally married to one of his sons. She was carrying his grandchild. That thought shocked him momentarily. The child would be *his* grandchild, too, which would set up a relationship of sorts between himself and Galt whether he liked the idea or not. They would both be the child's grandparents. The thought left a sour taste in his mouth.

He turned and went into the house. Since Lena wasn't here to cook tonight he knew he'd have to do it himself. He didn't want to eat his sons' cooking. His own was bad enough.

He sliced a slab of bacon and dumped the slices into a pan. He peeled potatoes, sliced them, and dumped them into another pan. He poured some of the bacon grease over them. Lena had baked earlier in the week and there was plenty of bread. He got out a loaf and put it on the long table.

His sons began coming in. Clem was first, followed by Nate and Leon. Ross was last. When they were all seated, Guy put the food on the table and sat down. He helped himself first and his sons waited until he had.

When all had served themselves, Guy said: "After supper, we're all goin' in to town. Galt ran Lena off and we're goin' to take her back to him."

Ross said stubbornly: "She says she ain't goin' to go."

Guy scowled at him. "She'll go, all right. She ain't never crossed me before and she ain't goin' to do it now."

"But what if she won't?"

"Then I'll hogtie her like a calf." Guy was getting angry now, but he didn't realize it was because Ross was giving voice to his own unspoken doubts.

When supper was finished, they washed the dishes, then went outside and saddled up. The sun was down, the clouds stained with its last rays. All shoved rifles into their saddle scabbards. Guy put the shotgun into his. He knew that while you could scare a man with a rifle, you could terrify the same man with a scatter-gun. He led out toward town and his sons fell in behind.

They reached town at 8:00 P.M. Guy turned his head and looked at Ross. "Where was she when you seen her last?"

"At Sherm Gatewood's house."

"She's stayin' there? Why not at the hotel?"

Ross shook his head. "I don't know. Probably because she don't have no money."

"Pres might've given her some."

Nobody said anything. After a moment Guy said: "We'll go to Gatewood's."

The five drew their horses to a halt in the street outside the little house. Nobody tied.

For a moment Guy sat there, staring at the lighted window of the house. Then he said: "Be quiet. No use getting' Gatewood mixed up in this."

Guy dismounted and, handing his reins to Ross, said: "You stay here and hold 'em. This ain't going to take very long."

The others followed suit.

Clem whispered: "You ain't goin' to hurt her, are you, Pa?"

Guy growled: "Long as she does what she's told, nothin's going to happen to her."

He peered in the window. Lena sat in a chair, staring straight ahead. There was a scared, discouraged look about her. Guy walked to the door and knocked. He heard Lena's footsteps and a moment later the door opened.

Guy didn't wait for an invitation but walked right in. Lena backed away from the door. The scared look was gone from her eyes. In its place was a defiant one. She asked coldly: "What do *you* want?"

Guy said, "Ain't right for a new bride to be spendin' her wedding night all alone like this. Where's Pres?"

"Out at the ranch, I suppose."

"What do you mean, you suppose? Don't you know?"

"All right," she said wearily. "He's out at the ranch."

"Why ain't you out there with him?"

"Galt told me to leave."

"And you left?"

"What else could I do? I can't fight the whole lot of them."

"You got a legal right to be out there."

She swung around and faced him, fury in her eyes, her face drawn and white. Angrily she said: "I don't care what kind of right I have. I don't *want* to be out there. I don't *want* to be married to Pres. I'm not going to be used as a weapon in your fight with Galt. I let you bully me this morning because I was scared and because I didn't know what else to do. But not any more. I'm through. I'm through with Pres and I'm through with you. From now on I'm going to live my own life the way I see fit."

For an instant Guy looked startled. Then the color began to seep into his face. His eyes narrowed and his jaws clenched. His voice came out like a rumble. "Don't you talk to me like that."

"Then get out of my house."

"Your house? This is Gatewood's house."

"He's letting me use it until I find something else."

"And how are you payin' him? God damn you, Lena, you're just like your mother was. You're a slut! You. . . ."

He didn't finish. White-faced now, Lena swung her hand. It struck him on the cheek with a suddenness that froze all movement in the room. Guy's face had been red with anger. Now it paled, leaving the red mark of Lena's hand upon his cheek. He lunged at her, grappling, but moving as quickly as a deer, she eluded him. Guy roared. "Get her, dammit! Grab her!"

None of his sons moved. Guy could see the triumph of this morning slipping away from him. If Lena let them get by with driving her away, Galt Majors would have little trouble getting the marriage set aside. He could claim coercion, force. He could ruin Lena's reputation by claiming the child wasn't Pres's child. He could make a laughingstock of Guy all over the county. No, by God, Lena had to go back to the Majors Ranch. It was the only way.

He plunged across the room after her. She stood poised against the wall, ready to jump either way, knowing she was quicker than her father but knowing also that he would catch her eventually unless she escaped out the door.

His hand brushed her arm as she darted aside. Guy whirled, roaring at his sons: "Catch her!"

Clem moved to block the door. Lena, heading for it, swerved sharply. She slipped as she did and fell.

For an instant nobody moved. Lena lay sprawled awkwardly on the floor, conscious, but obviously hurt.

Guy stood over her, ready to grab her if she tried to get away again. But Lena showed no signs of getting up. Her face was twisted with intense pain.

Suddenly she drew her knees up closer to her chest. Her face twisted more violently. She screamed, the scream literally wrenched from her. She twisted, and rolled, and screamed again.

Shocked, Guy stared down at her. Clem and Leon and Nate looked as shocked as their father did. The door slammed open and Gatewood stood framed in it. "What the hell is going on in here?"

Guy stared dumbly at him. Gatewood knelt at Lena's side. He could see the way pain twisted her face and narrowed her eyes as it came in waves. He slid his arms under her and lifted her. He carried her to the couch and laid her down on it. Turning, he said: "Don't just stand there. Go get Doc Simms."

Guy said: "She don't need no doc. She probably just wrenched some muscles as she fell."

Gatewood crossed the room. He was as tall as Guy if not as thick. His eyes were furious. "This is my house. Get out of it!"

"I. . . ."

"God damn you, I said get out of here!"

Guy tried to hold Gatewood's glance and failed. Grumbling, he turned and shuffled out the door, followed by his sons. Gatewood slammed the door and returned to the couch. He said: "I'll get the doc for you. I'll only be gone a couple of minutes. Will you be all right?"

There was perspiration on her forehead and upper lip. She nodded weakly, almost instantly convulsed as another spasm of pain knifed through her. Gatewood turned and ran, taking time to lock the door behind him. Guy might be stupid enough to come back. He might even be stupid enough to try taking her away with him.

Doc Simms lived two blocks away. Gatewood ran all the way. He banged on Doc's door and Doc came almost immediately, a pipe in his hand. Gatewood said: "It's Lena Dymond, Doc. She'd down at my place. Hurry, will you?"

Doc turned, got his hat, coat, and bag, and came right out. Gatewood wanted to run all the way back, too, but he knew Doc wouldn't run. He forced himself to walk, but his walk was so swift that Doc had trouble keeping up. Puffing slightly, he asked: "What's the matter with Lena, Sherm?"

"She fell. I guess you know by now. I guess everybody does. She's. . . ."

Doc said: "I know. I saw her on the hotel verandah today."

They reached Gatewood's little house. Guy and his sons sat their horses in front of it. Doc went in and Gatewood looked up at Guy. "Get out of here."

Guy opened his mouth to argue, then changed his mind. Sullenly he turned his horse and headed for the saloon, his sons following. Gatewood sat down on the porch steps and stared after them, more scared than he had been in a long, long time.

VIII

Guy Dymond dismounted in front of the saloon. His sons pulled up behind him, dismounting, too. Guy tramped inside, his four sons following along close behind.

Dutch Hoffman, who seldom saw any of the Dymonds in his saloon, nodded cordially. " 'Evenin', Mister Dymond. What's it going to be?"

"Whiskey. Give us the bottle." Guy laid a dollar on the bar.

Dutch put a bottle on the bar, along with five glasses. Guy dumped a generous portion into his own glass and shoved the bottle to Clem, standing next to him.

Lena had been screaming and carrying on unnecessarily, he thought sourly. Probably just trying to bring Gatewood into it. He'd never heard of anybody being hurt by falling down.

But Lena's screaming had convinced him of one thing. He wasn't going to be able to force her to go back out to the Majors Ranch. Taking her there by force would be useless, because she would simply return to town at the first opportunity. Nor could he force Galt Majors to accept her against his will. He had forced Pres to marry her, but that was as far as it was going to go.

He gulped his whiskey, and poured himself another drink. Dammit, he wasn't going to give up that easily. Today had been a day of triumph for him. Once more he savored what it had felt like, shoving Galt's face into the dirt. No, sir. He wasn't going to let triumph be turned into defeat. Not if he could help it. Not without trying, anyway.

Clem, standing next to him, asked: "Pa, what you goin' to do?"

Guy shook his head. "I don't know yet. But, by God, I ain't goin' to quit. Somehow or other we're goin' to make that son-of-a-bitch take her in."

"She says she ain't goin to go."

"I know that's what she says. But you know how women are. They say one thing and mean another. She'll go out there, but they'll have to make her feel like she's welcome. Like she belongs."

"They'll never do that. Not in a thousand years."

Guy's anger stirred at Clem's positive tone. "What the hell do you know about it anyway? You don't know what makes Galt Majors tick, and, by God, I do."

"You think you can scare him?"

"I know damn' well I can scare him. I did it once, twenty-five years ago. Far as I know, he never chased another woman after I put that bullet in his gut. The same thing will work this time."

Clem frowned worriedly. "This is different, Pa. You can't go around shootin' people just because they won't do what you want them to. Galt's rich and he's got a lot of influence. You shoot him and you'll go to jail."

"I got off last time and I will this time, too."

"Pa, can't you see? This is different."

"Uhn-uh. It ain't different. Besides, I ain't going to have to shoot Galt. All I got to do is make him think I will."

Clem stared at his father's set and angry face. He knew it wouldn't work. His father would have known it, too, if he'd been thinking straight. But he wasn't thinking straight. He'd hated Galt bitterly for twenty-five years. He'd watched Galt accumulate money and had watched his holdings grow while he himself continued to scratch out a bare living back in the hills.

Lena's pregnancy had given him a chance to get back at Galt, and he'd taken it. The trouble was it had backfired. And if Guy went on with it, he was going to end up in real trouble. Maybe in jail. Maybe even on the gallows.

Staring at his father's set and angry face, Clem knew he wasn't going to listen to anything anybody had to say. He shrugged, picked up his drink, and gulped it down.

Guy said: "Let's go."

Ross and Leon and Nate glanced at him. "Go where?" Nate asked.

"Out there to Galt Majors's place. He ain't goin' to get away with treatin' Lena like dirt. Not whilst I'm alive."

Nate said: "Pa, that's crazy. What we done last night was bad enough. But this. . . ."

Guy's eyes blazed. "You'll do what I tell you to!"

Clem could see that the only effect of Nate's argument had been to firm Guy's resolve. He shrugged, remaining silent. He poured another drink and gulped it down. He turned toward the door. There was doubt in the faces of the two younger brothers but they knew that, if Nate and Clem couldn't change their father's mind, they'd be wasting their time to try.

Meekly the four followed Guy out into the night. Silently they untied and mounted their horses and as silently followed Guy down the street and out of town. He rode at a steady trot, his chin resting on his chest. He was a big and bulky man, strong as an ox despite his age. Clem, riding behind him, knew they weren't going to ride in and surprise Galt Majors again. Galt would be expecting something like this if he had any sense. He knew Guy Dymond as well as Guy knew him. He knew Guy wouldn't have forced the marriage between Lena and Pres only to stand aside and do nothing when Lena was sent away.

Galt and his sons and the ranch crew would be waiting for them when they arrived. There'd be a gun battle, and it would end up with someone dead and the others charged with murder.

Behind him, Ross called: "Clem!"

Clem tightened his reins slightly and his horse dropped back, joining Ross fifty feet behind the others. Keeping his voice low, Ross said: "They'll be waitin' for us, sure as hell. It won't be as easy as it was last night."

"I know it won't."

"You know what he's up to, don't you?"

"What are you talkin' about? Sure I know what he's up to."

"I don't think you do. If old Galt was dead, Pres would own a quarter of the Majors Ranch. And Lena is Pres's wife."

Clem stiffened. He said loyally: "Pa ain't thinkin' about money."

"How do you know he ain't thinkin' about money? You saw the way he manhandled Galt this morning in town. He was just darin' Galt to draw an' make a fight out of it."

Clem shook his head. "No he wasn't. He had that shotgun and he never gave Galt a chance to draw."

"Well, even if he didn't this morning, he gave Galt plenty of reason to hunt him up later an' make a fight of it."

Clem had to admit that, but he still didn't think Guy had even thought about the possibility of Lena's acquiring a share of the Majors Ranch through old Galt's death. He said stubbornly: "Connivin' for a share of Galt's ranch ain't like Pa."

"How do you know what Pa is like? He's hated Galt Majors for twenty-five years. He's watched Galt get rich whilst he kept gettin' poorer all the time. The truth is, he don't give a damn whether Lena's kid has a name or not. He forced that marriage just to get under old Galt's hide."

"Even if he did, it don't mean he's got any ideas about gettin' his hands on part of the Majors Ranch."

Ross was silent for a moment. Then he said: "I done a little figgerin' this morning. Galt's got ten thousand cattle on that ranch. At thirty dollars a head, that's three hundred thousand dollars. Think of it."

Clem thought of it. It was a staggering sum. It staggered his imagination. He'd never had more than $30 at one time in his entire life.

Ross said: "Say the land is worth as much as the cattle, that makes the whole shebang worth six hundred thousand. And a fourth of that is a hundred and fifty thousand. Think of it, Clem. Think of it."

Clem thought of it. $150,000! And it *was* within their reach. He wondered if his father had thought of it. He wondered if it was what Guy really had in mind. He said gruffly: "That's crazy talk. It'll never happen. Galt would have to be dead and so would Pres."

"Might happen out there tonight. It might. There's only one thing, though. Galt would have to be the first to die."

Clem touched heels to his horse's sides. The animal forged ahead. Clem called back: "I wouldn't let Pa hear you talkin' like that if I was you!"

He pulled up behind his father's bulky shape. He tried to put the conversation with Ross out of his mind but found that he could not. Those fantastic figures kept dancing before his eyes. $150,000! Despite his efforts not to do so, he could not help dividing $150,000 by six. It came to $25,000. That was the amount each of them would get if it were to be divided equally.

He shook himself angrily. $25,000 each wouldn't do them

any good if they were dangling from a rope. Or sitting in a prison cell. But however hard he tried to dismiss the whole thing from his mind, it hung there, tormenting him by its presence. He cursed Ross sourly, beneath his breath.

Guy turned his head. "What was Ross talkin' about?"

"Nothin', Pa."

"What do you mean nothin'? What did he say?"

Reluctantly Clem said: "He thinks you're after a share of the Majors Ranch. He said, if Galt was dead, Pres would have a quarter interest in the ranch. And if Pres was dead. . . ."

"Lena would have it, huh?"

"That's what Ross said. I told him you wasn't thinkin' about that."

"How do you know what I'm thinkin' about?"

"I guess I don't, Pa."

Guy said: "I hadn't thought about it, and that's the truth."

"I didn't think you had."

Guy was silent a moment, then he said thoughtfully: "Tantalizin', though, ain't it?"

Clem said: "That money wouldn't do us a damn' bit of good if we was hung. Or if we was sittin' in a prison cell."

"Nope. It wouldn't, would it?"

Ahead, Clem could suddenly see the dark bulk of the buildings, surrounded by towering trees. He said: "There it is."

"I see it."

"What you goin' to do?"

"Don't know yet. Ain't made up my mind." He turned in at the lane, calling softly: "Shut the gate, Ross."

Their horses made a clop-clop sound as they walked down the hard-packed road. Clem wondered if Guy was going to ride in openly like this, daring the defenders to shoot at them. He turned his head and looked at Guy, but it was too dark to tell what Guy's expression was. Clem guessed he'd have to wait.

They got to within a hundred yards of the house before the shot rang out. Guy stopped immediately. Softly he said: "Off your horses. Scatter to left and right. Keep hidden but keep your guns ready."

Instantly the four brothers left their horses. Clem and Ross went to the right, Nate and Leon to the left. Guy stayed where he was. A voice called: "Who is it and what do you want?"

"It's Guy Dymond! I want to talk to Galt!"

"He don't want to talk to you! He ain't got nothin' to say to you!" Clem thought the voice was that of Len Peabody, Galt's foreman.

"He'll talk to me! If he's got any guts, he will!"

There was silence for a moment, and then Galt's harsh voice shouted: "Well, what do you want?"

"I want you to take Lena back. She's your daughter-in-law. Legally. She's got a right."

"She ain't got no rights! Not out here!"

Guy shouted: "You recollect what I done to you twenty-five years ago?"

Again that silence, but at last Galt shouted: "I recollect!"

"You take her back, or I'll do it again! I swear to God I will!"

Galt yelled: "You're outnumbered at least two to one! Get out of here while you can!"

Guy was already leaving the saddle as he yelled: "You had your chance!" He hit the ground running and dived into the ditch at the side of the road. A volley racketed down beside the house, but it must have been aimed high, because none of the five horses was hit. They were frightened, though, enough to turn and trot up the lane.

Guy called softly to his sons: "All right, let's move in on 'em. Let's see if they can fight as well as they can talk." He got to his feet as he spoke and let go with one barrel of the shotgun, immediately afterward hitting the dirt again. Clem could hear the buckshot rattling against the roof of the house. He could see the flashes of the defenders' guns and could hear their reports, sounding sharply after the deep-throated roar of the scatter-gun. He couldn't see what Guy hoped to accomplish and he couldn't see how the five of them could come out of this alive, let alone win. But Guy was his father. Leon and Nate and Ross were his brothers. He'd stay with them and fight because he had no other choice.

IX

Gatewood knew, if Guy did not, that Lena's condition was serious. His own mother had miscarried after a fall when he was five years old.

He angrily watched Guy Dymond and his four sons until they disappeared into the saloon. Not a one of them had given a thought to how Lena felt.

He stared gloomily in the direction of the saloon. Guy was stubborn and dangerous, he thought. His sons were younger replicas of their father. They would do what he told them to even if it led them straight to the gallows or the penitentiary.

How had Lena come from such a family? he wondered. She was all the things her father and brothers weren't. She must have learned from her mother, he thought, while Guy's sons learned from him. It was the only explanation that made any sense.

He could hear her talking with Doc Simms inside the house. He could hear Doc's deep voice occasionally. And sometimes he would hear a sharp cry of pain, a groan, or a quickly indrawn breath.

He got up and began to pace nervously back and forth. He must be a strange one, he thought. Lena's pregnancy, particularly out of wedlock and by another man, should have made him lose interest in her if not compassion for her plight. It had not. He found himself wishing he had not been so childishly stubborn after the quarrel they'd had. He should have seen her again. He should have continued their relationship. If he had, she would not now be in this fix.

He heard the door open and swung around to face it. Doc came out, closing the door quietly behind him. Gatewood said impatiently: "Well?"

"She's had a nasty fall. In her condition it could be serious. I've given her some laudanum to quiet her and reduce the pain, but I can't tell what's going to happen for a while."

"You're not leaving, are you?"

"I'm going to get Missus Campbell to stay the night with her."

"She's going to be all right, isn't she?"

"I think so, Sherm, but it's too soon to tell. She may lose the child."

Gatewood asked: "Should I go in and stay with her while you're gone?"

Doc nodded. "I wish you would. She shouldn't be alone."

Doc walked up the street, carrying his little bag. Gatewood went quietly into the house.

Lena lay on the couch, covered with a blanket. Her face was excessively pale. Her eyes were closed. Gatewood said softly: "Lena?"

Her eyes opened and she turned her head. Tears suddenly filled her eyes and ran across her cheeks. Gatewood crossed the room and sat down beside the couch. He found her hand and held it in both his own. He said: "Doc went to get Missus Campbell to stay with you."

She nodded listlessly. Behind her tears there was a hopeless expression as if she didn't care whether she lived or died. Gatewood didn't know what to say. He wanted to say something that would make her feel better but he didn't know what it would be. He was afraid that whatever he did say would come out wrong.

She asked weakly: "Where's Pa?"

"Down at the saloon."

"Then he hasn't gone home?"

"Not yet."

"Don't let him. . . ." She couldn't go on.

Gatewood said: "He won't bother you again. You have my word for that."

She smiled faintly, and her hand squeezed his weakly. He felt his throat tightening up.

She asked: "Where's Pres?"

"Out at the ranch, I suppose." She did not reply and he asked: "Do you want me to get him?"

She shook her head.

"Is there anything I can get for you?"

Again she shook her head. Faintly then, so faintly that he scarcely heard, she said: "I'm sorry, Sherm."

"Sorry? It should have been me that made up after that quarrel. I'm the one that ought to be sorry, not you. I kept thinking I would, and then I kept putting it off, and then you were going with Pres and it was too late."

Her eyes were closed. She nodded her head. Suddenly her face twisted as the pain knifed through her again. Her hand squeezed his, her fingernails digging in.

He looked helplessly at the door, wondering where Doc was, or Mrs. Campbell. He asked worriedly: "You want me to go get Doc again?"

There was sweat on her forehead and her hand was damp. "No. I'll be all right." Gradually her face relaxed, leaving her very pale.

Gatewood said: "Lena, when you get over this. . . ."

Weakly she shook her head. "You're just feeling sorry for me now. It's too late, Sherm."

"No it isn't. It's never too late if. . . ." He stopped, knowing this was no time to settle anything. It was no time to upset her by arguing. He said: "We'll talk about it when you're feeling all right again."

She did not reply. He heard footsteps on the porch and turned his head. The door opened and Mrs. Campbell came in.

She was a broad, motherly-looking woman, but strictly a no-nonsense type. She nodded to him, her glance telling him he could leave now that she was here. He released Lena's hand and said: "I'll see you tomorrow, Lena."

Lena nodded faintly. Her eyes were on Mrs. Campbell and she looked as if she expected to be scolded. Mrs. Campbell said comfortingly: "Dearie, you just close your eyes and try to sleep. You're going to be all right."

Gatewood opened the door and went outside. He stood for a moment with his back to the door, fumbling for his pipe and tobacco. Deliberately he packed the pipe and lit it.

The rail in front of the saloon had only two horses tied to it. Gatewood released a long sigh of relief. At least the Dymonds had had sense enough to go on home.

It had been a long day, he thought, beginning before daylight when he was awakened by Galt Majors and Guy. He walked to the saloon and went inside. Dutch Hoffman was behind the bar. Ernie was sweeping. Both glanced up as he came in.

Two cowboys were at a table in the corner. Otherwise the place was empty. Gatewood crossed to the bar and Dutch said: " 'Evenin', Sheriff."

" 'Evenin', Dutch."

"What's it gonna be?"

"Whiskey. It's been a busy day for a sleepy little town like Cottonwood Springs."

Dutch grinned and set a bottle and glass in front of him.

Gatewood laid a dollar on the bar, then dumped a little whiskey in the glass. He gulped it down.

He couldn't get Lena's face out of his mind, pale, twisted with pain, sweating. She deserved better than Pres, he thought, then grinned wryly. By better than Pres, did he mean himself?

He knew he'd been a fool for letting Lena get away from him. He also knew he'd be glad to have her back. Anytime. Under any circumstances. But he'd let his chance slip away and now it was too late. Whatever he did now was sure to be misinterpreted, both by Lena and by the community as a whole.

He poured himself another drink and looked at Dutch. "Looks like Guy and his boys finally went home."

Dutch shook his head. "They didn't go home. They went out to the Majors place."

"They did what?"

"They went out to the Majors place. I heard 'em talkin' before they left. The boys were tryin' to talk Guy out of it, but you know how stubborn he can be. Said Galt was goin' to take Lena back or by God he was goin' to know why."

Gatewood groaned. If Guy went out to the Majors Ranch, there'd be a battle. It might turn into a full-scale range war before it could be stopped.

But he didn't move. Guy had probably changed his mind. Guy wasn't stupid, and going out to start trouble at the Majors Ranch was an exceedingly stupid thing to do.

He finished his second drink, waited for Dutch to make change, then went out into the night. He walked slowly to the jail, puffing thoughtfully on his pipe. He stopped in front of his house and stared at the dimly lit window. Mrs. Campbell must have turned the lamp down very low. He listened, but he heard no sound.

He went into the jail, leaving the door open so that he could hear if Lena screamed. He sat down, but he couldn't stay down.

He got up and nervously began to pace back and forth again.

Suddenly he heard a single, piercing scream, muffled by the walls of his house, but unmistakably that of Lena, unmistakably a scream of terrible pain. He started toward the house, was halfway there when the door opened.

Mrs. Campbell stood framed in it. "Get the doctor, Mister Gatewood. Hurry!"

Gatewood turned and ran toward Doc Simms's house. Reaching it, he slammed open the gate, ran up on the porch, and pounded violently on the door.

Doc opened it, hat on, coat in one hand, black bag in the other. He came out immediately. He handed Gatewood the bag, shrugged into his coat as he hurried down the street. When he could talk, he asked: "Missus Campbell send you for me?"

"Yeah. Lena was screaming again."

"I'm afraid she's . . . going to . . . lose her child." Doc was out of breath already.

"What about her, Doc? Is she going to be all right?"

"Too soon to know."

They reached Gatewood's house and Doc went inside. Gatewood waited outside, wincing every time Lena screamed or moaned. And after each sound she made, he softly cursed Pres beneath his breath. Or he cursed old Galt for sending her away. Or he cursed Guy for trying to force her to go back out there.

Time dragged with maddening slowness. Half an hour passed. An hour. He realized suddenly that there hadn't been a sound from the house for more than three quarters of an hour now. He wondered if Lena had died, and he felt his throat tightening just at the thought.

At last the door opened. Doc came out onto the porch. He was in his shirt sleeves, which were rolled up above his elbows. His hair was mussed and he looked very tired. He closed the door behind him.

Gatewood rushed toward him. "Well? Is she all right?"

"She's sleeping," Doc said wearily.

"I asked you if she was all right. I want a better answer from you than that."

Doc peered at him. "That's right. You did go with her for a while, didn't you? What happened?"

Gatewood said fiercely: "Doc, damn you, if you don't give me an answer. . . ."

Doc said: "She'll be all right, Sherm. But she lost the child."

Gatewood felt a long, slow sigh escape his lips.

Doc said: "She'll have to stay in bed for at least a week. I'll leave Missus Campbell here to take care of her. Just don't let her father take her home. Do you understand? I'll look in on her tomorrow."

"Don't worry, Doc. I won't let Guy get near to her."

"All right." Doc went back inside, reappeared a moment later with his coat and hat and bag. Again he let Gatewood hold his bag while he put on his coat. He said—"Good night."—wearily and trudged away toward home.

Gatewood stared at the house. He realized that he was shaking. He realized suddenly how terribly scared he had been.

He suddenly didn't care who misinterpreted what. As soon as Lena was well he was going to start seeing her again. And as soon as it was possible, he was going to ask her to marry him.

In the meantime, Guy and her brothers and Galt and Pres had better let her alone. Unless they wanted to tangle with him.

He walked slowly to the jail, went inside, and closed the door. He laid down on the cot without even removing his boots. He was tired but he knew he wouldn't sleep. Not for a while. And besides, he had an uneasy feeling that this day wasn't over with.

X

He was right about the day not being over with. He had been lying on his office couch less than five minutes when he heard the distant pound of hoofs. They grew louder steadily. By the time he reached the door, a rider was pulling his lathered horse to a halt just outside the jail.

Gatewood stepped out, peering through the darkness, trying to see who the rider was. He knew the minute he heard his voice. "Sheriff?"

It was Len Peabody, Galt Majors's foreman. Gatewood said: "It's me. What do you want?"

"You'd better get out to the Majors Ranch right away. There's a battle going on."

Gatewood cursed disgustedly beneath his breath. Damn Guy Dymond anyway. It didn't look like he was ever going to let it drop. He apparently wasn't going to quit until somebody got killed. He said: "All right. I'm coming." He went back into the jail and got his hat. He got a double-barreled ten-gauge shotgun from the rack, got a handful of shells for it out of the drawer of his desk. He shrugged into a coat and went back outside.

"Go down to the livery barn and have Buck saddle up a horse for me. I'll be along."

Peabody clattered away. Gatewood went to the door of his house and knocked softly. Mrs. Campbell opened it slightly and he said: "I've got to leave town for a little while. Will you be all right?"

"Don't worry about us."

"Is Lena still all right?"

"She's asleep."

He nodded, turned, and hurried toward the livery barn. By the time he reached it, his horse was saddled and ready. Peabody stood in the street, holding the reins of both horses. Gatewood swung astride and followed Peabody out of town.

Peabody rode at a canter. Gatewood drew abreast. "Has anybody been hurt?" he asked.

"Hadn't when I left. But the way the lead's flyin' around out there, it ain't goin' to be very long."

"Galt send you for me?"

"Nobody sent me. I came on my own."

Gatewood gave up trying to talk. The two thundered through the night. After a while, Gatewood's curiosity got the best of him and he yelled: "What'd Guy do, just ride in and begin shooting?"

"No. He called out that he wanted to talk to Galt. When Galt came out, Guy told him to take Lena back or he was goin' to shoot him again like he did twenty-five years ago."

"And then he started shooting?"

It was several moments before Peabody replied. "No. I guess it was us that started shootin' first. Does it matter?"

Gatewood couldn't see that it did. Guy had been trespassing and threatening and Galt had obviously believed he meant what he said. He yelled: "No! I can't see that it makes any difference."

They reached the Majors Ranch at last. From the gate above the house, Gatewood could hear the desultory popping of guns. He could see flashes both at the house and in the hay field between the gate and the house. Peabody asked: "What are you goin' to do?"

"I don't know, but I don't want you with me. Can you get back to the house without running into Guy or one of his sons?"

"Sure. I can go in the same way I came out, along the bed of Coyote Creek."

"Do it, then. Tell Galt I'm here. Tell him to stop shooting when he hears me yell."

"All right," Peabody said doubtfully. "I guess you know what you're doin'."

74

"I know." Gatewood watched him ride away, watched him fade into the darkness and disappear. He hadn't dared use Peabody to help him because he knew Guy could then accuse him of taking sides with Galt. He'd have to do this alone and he'd probably get shot doing it.

He opened the gate and went through, closing it behind him. The horses the Dymonds had ridden here were bunched just inside, their reins trailing, cropping grass.

He rode down the lane, wondering how close he could get before he was heard. Unless he called out, they'd probably think he was one of the Majors bunch and open up on him.

The whole thing was so stupid, he thought disgustedly. Guy wasn't going to force Galt to take Lena back. There was no way in the world that could be done. Lying here in the hay field in the middle of the night shooting at the house was even more stupid because sooner or later someone would get hurt or killed and then whoever was responsible would either be hanged or imprisoned.

When he judged he was as close as he dared to go, Gatewood halted and yelled: "Guy! Can you hear me, Guy?"

The shooting stopped suddenly down at the house. After a moment, Gatewood yelled again: "I know you can hear me, Guy! Answer me!"

Once more only silence greeted him. He felt a rash anger stirring in his mind. He was tired. He'd been awakened before dawn this morning. He'd had nothing but trouble with the Dymonds and the Majorses all day long. Now to be dragged up here in the middle of the night and to have Guy Dymond refuse to answer him made him furious. He bawled: "Damn you, Guy, answer me! Or, by God, I'm coming after you!"

Still no answer came to him out of the darkness ahead. All shooting had stopped, so he knew they had heard him and were listening. He also knew nothing had happened to Guy to prevent him from answering. If it had, Guy's sons would have let him know soon enough.

If Gatewood had stopped to think, he probably wouldn't have done it. But he didn't stop to think. He just surrendered to his anger and let it direct his action. He sank spurs into his horse's sides and thundered straight down the lane.

Someone let out a startled yell, and a gun flared. Another flared and another still, but they were shooting in the dark. They could neither see their sights nor, clearly, the target they were shooting at.

The flashes of their guns, however, told him where they were. A dozen yards from the nearest one, Gatewood left his horse, shotgun in hand, hitting the ground running.

His horse, a livery stable animal and poorly trained, did not stop as he left the saddle but continued to run. Gatewood heard a high bawl as the horse overran one of the Dymonds and heard the man's frantic scrambling and angry cursing as he tried to get out of the way.

Gatewood himself crashed into one of the others, and he brought the shotgun barrel savagely and efficiently sideways against the side of the man's head. The man crumpled without a sound.

Gatewood, still running headlong, caught the shape of yet another man immediately ahead of him. Another of Guy's sons, he knew, for the bulk of this one was not as great as that of Guy. Again his shotgun barrel did its angry work and again Gatewood went on.

Another figure loomed up ahead and he knew instantly that this one was Guy. Guy had either a rifle or shotgun in his hands, and was bringing it to bear. Gatewood shouted quickly, his own finger tight against the trigger: "Don't do it, Guy, or I'll cut you in two!"

He skidded to a halt, less than twenty feet away. He could kill

Guy from here with a pattern of buckshot that simply couldn't miss, and he would, if he thought Guy was going to shoot.

He said: "It's a double-barreled ten-gauge and I can't miss. Even if you shoot me, I can't miss."

For what seemed an eternity the two stood there, facing each other. Then Guy growled angrily—"Damn you, Gatewood!"—and lowered his gun but without letting go of it. Gatewood said—"Drop it!"—and Guy Dymond did.

Gatewood stepped forward and picked it up. He said: "Two of your sons are probably out cold but you can call in the other two."

Guy called: "Come on, boys! Come on over here. No shooting. It's the sheriff and he's got a gun on me."

Gatewood heard their shuffling steps rustling through the grass. He waited until they reached him. Then he directed them to drop their guns. They complied without argument.

Gatewood got behind Guy and jammed the shotgun muzzle into his back. He said: "Let's go."

"What about the boys?"

"These two can pack the other two."

"What about Galt and his men? Without me. . . ."

Gatewood raised his voice. "Galt?"

"What do you want?"

"I've got Guy. His boys may take a few minutes pulling out. No shooting, do you understand?"

There was no reply. Gatewood yelled: "Galt?"

"All right. As long as they don't shoot at us."

"Anybody hurt down there?"

"One of the hands got a bullet in the leg."

"Is it bad?"

"Bad enough. Send out the doc when you get to town."

"All right."

Galt shuffled heavily ahead of him. Gatewood didn't even

consider going back for his horse. He'd use one of the Dymonds' horses. They could use his. If they couldn't find the animal, they could ride double on one of theirs. The horse would get back to the livery stable by himself.

Guy reached the gate. Gatewood said: "Open it."

Guy did. Gatewood caught one of the horses and swung to his back. Guy mounted another one. He led out through the gate without a backward glance. They had covered almost a mile before he spoke. "What are you going to do with me?"

"I guess that'll depend on what kind of charges Galt wants to file."

"You mean you're goin' to put me in jail and keep me there until you find out?"

"That's what I mean. You've caused enough trouble for one day. I'm going to make sure you don't cause any more tomorrow."

"It ain't my doin'. It's Galt. And that god-damn' Pres."

"Sure. Blame everything on them."

"Well, ain't it? Pres is the one that got Lena in a family way. If it wasn't for me, she'd have had the brat without even botherin' to give it a name."

Gatewood felt his anger rising again. He clenched his jaws, trying to hold back all the things he wanted to say.

Guy said: "Now, by God, she's Pres's wife. And they're goin' to take her in. I'll see to that before I'm through."

Gatewood's anger spilled over for the second time tonight. He said furiously: "You're through using her as a weapon against Galt. She fell tonight when you were trying to force her to come out here with you. She lost the baby that you've been so concerned about. And in case you don't know it, she damned near lost her life."

"Just from fallin' down? The hell she did."

Gatewood clenched his teeth.

Guy said: "I thought Indian women was supposed to be tough. Sure looks like Lena ain't, don't it now?"

Gatewood said: "Shut up! Shut your mouth before I lay this shotgun barrel across it!"

"What the hell you gittin' so riled up about? This all ain't none of your never mind. It's a family matter. Why the hell don't you just mind your own business an' keep your nose out of ours?"

"Lena *is* my business."

"Not no more, she ain't. You had your chance. Right now she's Pres's wife an' that makes her part of the Majors family. She's got rights an' I aim to see she gets 'em."

Gatewood said softly: "I'll tell you just one more time. Shut up."

So much deadly emphasis was in his voice that Guy quickly turned his head, trying to see well enough to make out the expression on his face. He opened his mouth to say something, closed it again without doing so. Guy had been around long enough to know that it doesn't pay to poke a rattlesnake with a stick.

XI

Clem and Ross Dymond stood motionlessly in the hay field until they heard the gate squeak at the head of the lane. Then Clem said softly: "Can you find your gun?"

Ross said: "I think so." He stooped and retrieved his gun. Clem searched around and finally recovered his. He said: "That damn' Gatewood must've knocked Leon an' Nate both out with his gun. Go on up to the gate and get the horses. Bring 'em down here."

He could see the dim shape of Gatewood's horse standing between him and the Majors house. He debated going after the horse, decided against it. The animal was close to the house and it was too risky going after him. They'd make do with what they had.

He found Nate. Thirty feet away from him he located Leon. Nate was still out cold. Leon was groaning, sitting up and rubbing the side of his head. He grunted: "What happened?"

"Gatewood hit you with his gun. He hit Nate, too. Then he took Pa back to town."

"What are we supposed to do?"

"We're goin' to get out of here as soon as Ross comes back with the horses."

"What about Galt?"

"He agreed not to shoot at us as long as we don't shoot at him."

Leon stumbled to his feet, holding his head with both hands. "Where is Nate?"

"Over there." Both men stumbled through the darkness to where Nate lay. Clem heard Ross coming with the horses and called out to him.

While Leon held one of the horses, Ross and Clem lifted Nate and laid him, belly down, across the saddle. Clem loosened his belt and then hooked it over the saddle horn. Leon asked: "He ain't dead, is he?"

"Uhn-uh. He's breathin'." Clem mounted behind his brother. The other two mounted and followed him, Leon groaning occasionally from the throbbing pain in his head.

At the gate, Ross dismounted and opened it. He left it open, in this petty way trying to get back at Galt.

Halfway home, Nate recovered consciousness. Clem dismounted and eased him to the ground. When he had rested a few minutes and when things had been explained to him, he mounted. Clem swung up behind.

It was well past midnight when they reached home. Ross put the horses into the corral. The other three went into the house.

As he lit the lamp, Leon asked: "Do you think Gatewood will put Pa in jail?"

Clem said: "He sure as hell won't turn him loose. Not for a while at least."

"What are we goin' to do?"

Nobody answered him. Nate sat with his head down in both his hands. Leon seemed almost as sick. A trickle of blood had run down the side of his face from the wound at his temple and had dried.

Ross came in. He asked immediately: "What are we goin' to do?"

Clem frowned. He was the oldest and in Guy's absence it was up to him to decide. He said: "I reckon it's up to us to do what Pa wanted done."

"You mean make Galt take Lena back?"

"That's what I mean."

"How the hell are we supposed to do that?"

Clem frowned. He didn't know and he wasn't used to deciding things. Guy had always told them what he wanted done. Clem said: "Well, we can't make him take Lena back unless we can talk to him. And we can't talk to him unless we get him off by himself."

"How we goin' to do that?"

"We got to grab him when he's all alone. It's the only way I know."

"You mean we got to watch his house and get him when he leaves?"

"That's what I mean."

"You think that's what Pa would want?"

"Pa wants Galt to take Lena back. I don't reckon Pa cares much how it's done just so it gets done. Me an' Ross will get fresh horses an' ride over there while it's still dark. We'll hide in the brush up on the ridge behind the house. We'll stay there all

81

day tomorrow. You two can relieve us soon's it's good and dark tomorrow night."

Nate and Leon agreed with cautious nods. Clem got a bottle of his father's whiskey from its hiding place under his father's mattress. He took a drink and gave Ross one. He left the bottle for Nate and Leon, who, he figured, needed it worse than he and Ross did.

He filled a gunny sack with grub, got his blanket roll, and waited while Ross got his. The two went out into the darkness. The air was beginning to chill.

They got fresh horses out of the corral, saddled, and mounted up. They rode out, heading across country straight toward the Majors house.

It was near dawn when they arrived. Clem picketed the horses in a gully about half a mile from the Majors house. He didn't figure they'd be found. It was pretty rough where he left them and he doubted if the Majors hands ever came this way.

On foot, carrying the blankets and grub, the two made their way to the top of the ridge. From here they could look down at the ranch buildings. The house was less than a quarter mile away.

Clem was as tired as Ross, but he didn't want to take a chance on Ross falling asleep on watch so he said: "Stretch out. I'll keep an eye on things for a little while."

Ross didn't argue. He lay down and pulled his blanket over him. In a matter of minutes he was sound asleep. He snored, but Clem didn't bother him until his snores became loud enough to be heard by the sharp-eared dogs down below. When that happened, Clem nudged him with a foot.

Dawn came as a gray line along the eastern horizon. The sky gradually grew lighter and finally the clouds took on a pinkish hue. A door slammed down below and a few minutes later a plume of smoke rose from the kitchen chimney. Shortly afterward, smoke began to pour from the bunkhouse chimney, too.

A man came out of the bunkhouse, wearing only his long red underwear and boots. He scratched his belly and headed for the outhouse. He disappeared into it.

Another man, this one wearing pants, came out and headed for the pump. Its handle squeaked as he pumped enough water to wash. He stuck his head under the spout, straightened, and reached for the towel hanging from a post.

Clem rummaged in the grub sack. He got some bread and a jar of jam and had some breakfast. There was a canteen in the sack, so he drank from it. He wished he had coffee, but he did not.

Living wasn't going to be very easy without Lena at home, he thought. She had been a good cook. She had done their laundry and kept the house clean. With her gone, they'd have to do all those things for themselves. The meals would be terrible and the laundry wouldn't get done. The house would probably never get cleaned.

Down below, men came and went from the bunkhouse. The outhouse door slammed repeatedly. The pump handle squeaked every time somebody washed.

A slight breeze blew toward Clem from the house. He could smell bacon frying, and he could smell coffee. He finished eating and settled back. He wished he could go to sleep. He felt as if he wasn't going to be able to keep his eyes open a moment more.

He must have dozed. He snapped awake, hearing Ross utter a thunderous snore. He dug a foot into Ross's ribs. Ross grunted and turned over. Clem stared at the ranch buildings down below.

There was considerable activity at the corral as the hands caught horses out of the bunch that had, apparently, just been driven in. Dust still hung in the air between the corral and the pasture south of the house. Clem was able to pick out Len Peabody, standing in front of the corral handing out assignments for the day. He could hear Len's voice but he could only make out a few of his words. But he did hear one of the hands yell: "What about Guy Dymond?"

And he heard Len Peabody's reply: "Guy's in jail. He ain't goin' to bother us for a while."

In small groups, the hands rode away, scattering in all directions. Len Peabody went back into the bunkhouse, and for almost an hour there was no activity of any kind that Clem could see.

Then he stiffened. Galt Majors came from the house.

He stood on the back stoop and yelled for Peabody. When Peabody came to the bunkhouse door, Galt yelled: "Saddle my horse, Len!"

Peabody went to the corral. He caught a horse, took him to the barn, emerged a few moments later leading him, a saddle in place on his back. He led him to the back door of the house, and old Galt swung astride. They conversed several moments and then Galt rode away, turning south down the bed of Coyote Creek.

Clem knelt and shook Ross awake. "Let's go."

Ross got up sleepily and followed him to the gully where the horses were. They coiled picket ropes and mounted. Clem stayed in the hills as long as he could, then cut across the hay field to the creek, glancing occasionally toward the ranch buildings half a mile away. He saw no one and apparently no one saw him.

Galt must still be in the creek bottom, he decided, since he'd seen no one leaving it. Probably just poking along. They should be able to get well ahead of him, hide themselves, and then just wait until he came along. He was all alone. He wouldn't be stupid enough to put up a fight.

How he and Ross would persuade Galt to take Lena back Clem had no idea. He'd just have to try. It was what his father wanted, what his father would do it he was not in jail.

The bed of Coyote Creek was, perhaps, a quarter mile wide. Huge cottonwoods grew in it, and brush. Hidden by the high brush that grew at its edge, Clem and Ross rode south, not halting until they had covered several miles.

At a point where the Coyote Creek bottom narrowed down to less than two hundred yards, Clem dismounted and nodded at Ross to follow suit. They tied their horses and, on foot, backtracked for a hundred yards. Clem pointed out a spot where he wanted Ross to wait. He found himself another not far away. The way they were situated, Galt Majors could not ride past without being seen.

Now they only had to wait. But the waiting was very hard. Clem started every time a twig cracked and every time a bird flew past. Half an hour passed and he began to wonder if Galt Majors had not turned back.

Then, suddenly, he heard a crashing in the brush ahead. A buck deer came bounding toward him. He heard a stirring where Ross was and saw that Ross had raised his rifle. Clem called sharply: "Put that down!"

The deer heard him and saw the movement Ross had made. He veered sharply to one side, left the brushy creek bottom in great twenty-foot bounds, and headed across the hay field toward the hills. Clem caught Ross's eye and signaled for silence. Galt must have spooked the deer. If he had, he would be along before very long.

He was right. Less than five minutes had passed before Galt rode out of the heavy brush. He seemed to be deep in thought and there was a small frown on his face.

Clem nodded at Ross and got quickly to his feet, rifle held at the ready. He jacked a cartridge into the chamber and heard

Ross follow suit. Galt started violently and his horse, as startled as he was, shied.

Clem said: "Easy, Mister Majors. Just get down off your horse."

"What is the meaning of this?"

Clem's voice took on a little edge. "I said get down. We ain't fixin' to hurt you. We just want to talk."

"Talk? I've got nothing to say to you. And you'd both better put those guns down and get off my land or you'll find yourselves where your father is . . . in jail."

Clem said stubbornly: "Don't push me, Mister Majors. I told you to get down off your horse. Are you goin' to do it or do I have to pull you down the way Pa did yesterday?"

Galt hesitated, looking from one to the other. He was angry but he was also scared. "What do you want to talk about?"

"Lena. Pa wants you to take her back."

"She doesn't want to come. Even if I agreed to take her back, she wouldn't come."

His eyes kept darting back and forth, from Clem's face to Ross's. Clem risked a glance at Ross. Ross's face was all screwed up. His eyes were narrowed. He had raised his rifle until it was almost to his shoulder.

Clem realized with a shock that Ross was thinking about the money. He was thinking that if Galt was dead, Lena would have, with Pres, a one-fourth interest in the Majors Ranch.

He said sharply: "Ross! Put down that gun!"

Galt, who had also seen the way Ross was looking at him and the way his gun had raised, knew he was about to be shot. He sank spurs into his horse's sides, at the same time reining him sharply to the right. The horse leaped forward, turned, fighting the bit, and then plunged away through the brush.

Ross's rifle roared. Clem bawled—"Ross!"—but the excitement of the hunt was in Ross now. It was as if Galt and his horse were a deer Ross had spooked out of the brush. He fired, and levered, and fired again.

Galt was driven sideways off his horse. He hit in heavy brush with a crash. The horse, thoroughly terrified, plunged away through the brush, in seconds gaining the hay field where he could run unhampered and free.

Clem looked at Ross, whose gun still was smoking in his hands. He said: "You stupid son-of-a-bitch! What the hell did you do that for?"

Ross was running toward the place where Galt now lay. He panted: "He was tryin' to get away! You saw him! He was tryin' to get away!"

"That wasn't no reason to shoot him. Now what the hell are we goin' to do?"

He reached Galt's body where it lay, supported by the brush into which it had fallen. The front of Galt's shirt was soaked with blood. There was no movement in his chest.

Clem said: "Oh, God! He's dead."

Ross said: "A hundred and fifty thousand dollars. Think of it."

"What we'd better think about is gettin' the hell out of here." Clem turned and ran for his horse, hearing Ross crashing along behind.

There was a hopeless sense of shock in Clem. Something had been done that could never be undone. And because of it, there was going to be hell to pay.

XII

Dinner was on at noon, just as it always was. Donald, Robert, James, and Pres were all present, but Galt was not. Donald glanced at Pres as the youngest of the four pulled out a chair and sat down. "Where's Pa?"

"How the hell should I know? I don't keep track of him."

Donald walked to the kitchen door. He looked at Ling, the cook. "Did Pa tell you he wouldn't be back for dinner?"

"He no say nothing."

"What time did he leave?"

"He call Len Peabody early this morning to saddle horse."

"What time?"

"Mebbe eight, nine o'clock."

Donald frowned. He went through the kitchen and out the back door. He crossed the yard to the bunkhouse and went in. Peabody was sitting at the long table along with Hymie Meers, who did the chores, and Link McCracken, one of the hands. Donald asked: "Len, did Pa say where he was going?"

Peabody shook his head. "Ain't he back yet?"

"Uhn-uh. And he's always back for dinner unless he tells somebody different."

"He'll be back."

Donald nodded. "I suppose he will." He went out and looked around. Len Peabody came to the bunkhouse door, and Donald asked: "Which way did he go?"

"South. Down the bed of Coyote Creek."

Donald shrugged. "He'll probably be along." He went back to the house and disappeared inside.

Peabody stood in the bunkhouse doorway, staring south. Failing to show up for dinner was unusual for Galt. It made him wonder what might have happened to prevent the old man from getting back. Frowning, he went back into the bunkhouse and sat down. Red Muldoon, the cook, put a platter of meat in front of him and went back for the fried potatoes. Peabody helped himself and passed the platter on.

Halfway through the meal he got up and went to the door again. He glanced at the corral, up at the house, and down the bed of Coyote Creek. He did not see Galt.

He went back inside and sat down, scoffing at his own uneasiness. Guy Dymond was in jail and his sons had gotten their bellies full of fighting last night. There was nothing to worry about.

But he couldn't rid himself of the nagging feeling that something was wrong. When he had finished eating, he went to the corral and saddled a horse. He rode south, and, after casting back and forth for fifteen or twenty minutes in the brush-grown bed of Coyote Creek, he managed to pick up Galt's trail.

Trailing was next to impossible in the creek bottom, partly because of the heavy brush, partly because Galt rode in the water as much as he rode out of it, and because there were a lot of other trails. Peabody climbed his horse out of the creek bottom onto the hay field. He crossed it at a gallop and climbed the side of the nearest ridge.

From here he could see for miles. The creek wandered back and forth, appearing from a distance to be several times as wide as it really was. Peabody saw nothing.

He fished a sack of tobacco and papers from his pocket and rolled himself a cigarette. He lit it. Squinting through the smoke, he thought he saw something move a couple of miles down the creek. A deer, he thought. But he continued to watch, eyes narrowed against the glare of the noonday sun.

He saw it again, more plainly, and knew at once that it was not a deer. It was a horse. A saddled horse.

Peabody dug heels into his horse's sides. The horse plunged down the side of the ridge, turning not toward the riderless horse two miles down Coyote Creek, but back toward the house.

Reaching it, Peabody rode straight to the back door. "Hey! Anybody here?"

Two of Galt's sons, Pres and Robert, appeared in the kitchen door. Peabody said: "I spotted a riderless horse a couple of miles down Coyote Creek. One or two of you had better ride into town. Get Doc Simms and get Gatewood, too."

"How do you know . . . ?"

"If Galt's horse is loose, it means he's either hurt or that he's been shot. Get goin' now."

He turned away immediately and rode to the bunkhouse door. He yelled: "Link!"

Link came out and Peabody said: "Hitch up a buckboard. Put a featherbed in the back and come on down the west side of Coyote Creek. The old man's horse is loose and I think he's hurt."

Link ran toward the corral to catch a team. Peabody galloped out of the yard, heading south once more.

He had gone almost a mile before he caught sight of Galt's horse again. The animal had apparently been moving fairly steadily toward the ranch house, but it was equally apparent that he was in no hurry. He was grazing as he traveled, and the trailing reins further slowed his progress because he kept stepping on them.

Peabody caught him and got down off his horse. He looked the saddle over carefully on one side, and then the other. There were no spots of blood—nothing to indicate what had happened to Galt.

Peabody ran his hand absently over the horse's neck. Something felt rough, and he looked more closely. It appeared to be a spot of blood that had dried on the horse's smooth hide.

Leaving the horse where he was, he mounted again. For a while it was easy to backtrack him because he had left a plain trail in the uncut grass, which was almost a foot high. But he lost it eventually and was forced to return to the creek bottom where once more he had to cast back and forth for some time before he was able to pick up Galt's trail.

Following it was a tedious business. He had traveled less than half a mile when he heard shouting on his right. He answered the shouts and a few minutes later was joined by Donald and

James Majors.

Donald looked extremely worried. He asked: "Find anything?"

Peabody shook his head. "Trailing's hard in here."

"What if we were to go on ahead?"

Peabody shook his head. "Uhn-uh. You'd just mess up the trail. Where's the buckboard?"

"Back there where we found Galt's horse."

"Go get it. Bring it up to here."

Donald trotted his horse away and disappeared. James said: "What do you think has happened to him?"

Peabody did not reply. He glimpsed something ahead in the heavy brush, something that did not belong. Galt had been wearing a brown shirt and vest and the thing he had just glimpsed was brown.

He reined his horse toward it, touching his sides with his heels. The horse, catching a scent he didn't like, laid back his ears and balked. Peabody kicked him angrily, forcing him to go ahead.

It was Galt, all right. And Peabody knew the minute he saw him that the scent of blood was what had made the horse balk so. Galt's shirt front was a welter of drying blood. His face was waxy and his chest was still. He lay awkwardly, half on his back, half on his side, supported by a thick clump of brush into which he had fallen. Peabody called: "Here he is!"

James came immediately, dismounting as soon as he saw his father's body. "Is he . . . ?"

Peabody said: "He's dead."

"Oh my God! How . . . ?"

"Shot."

James reached the body and stood looking down at it, horror written in his face. Peabody said: "Go get the buckboard."

"What about tracks? What about . . . ?"

"We'll leave that for Gatewood. Long as we stay on this side of him, we won't mess anything up."

"Who . . . ?"

Peabody looked at him. Galt had been tough and strong, but his sons were weaklings. Maybe because old Galt had never let them be anything else. He said: "The Dymonds. Who else?"

"But Guy's in jail."

"Guy's got four sons. Go on now. Get the buckboard."

He hunkered down a few feet from the body and watched James get his horse, mount, and ride out of the brushy creek bottom. He had worked for Galt a dozen years, starting as a cowhand, working up as Galt put more and more trust in him. He hadn't liked Galt. He doubted if anyone had. But he had respected him. Galt had been tough as rawhide, ruthless and acquisitive, but he had been scrupulously honest, too. Peabody was sorry he was dead. As for avenging him, that was the sheriff's business.

He heard the buckboard before he saw it. He yelled—"Over here, Link!"

A few minutes later, he saw Link sitting up on the buckboard seat as it drew to a halt at the edge of the brush.

Link and James and Donald came pushing through the brush. Peabody helped them lift Galt's body and carry it to the buckboard. They laid it in back on the featherbed and covered it with a blanket Link had brought. Peabody said: "Go on back with it. I'll wait here."

No one questioned his order. Link drove out across the hay field, heading for the ranch house. Galt's sons fell in behind.

Peabody hunkered down at the edge of the hay field. He rolled himself a smoke and puffed it thoughtfully. He felt suddenly very lonely, as if some essential were missing from his life. It would be different without Galt. Easier in some ways, harder in others. The old man's sons might not want him around. Or,

92

on the other hand, they might depend on him more than they had when Galt was alive. But no matter what happened, Galt's death was bound to have a profound effect on his life.

Several times while he waited, he got up and paced nervously back and forth. He had used up all his tobacco before he saw Gatewood, riding toward him along the wheel tracks left in the hay by the buckboard.

Gatewood dismounted and dropped his horse's reins. "Hello, Len."

"Hello, Sherm."

"Where'd you find him?"

"Come on." Peabody led him to where the body had been sprawled in the brush. Carefully Gatewood walked beyond the place, studying the ground as he did. He found the tracks of the boots of two men beside the body, found a profusion of the same tracks beyond. Going on, he found droppings where their horses had been tied, and saw the trail that led away, both horses obviously galloping. He followed that trail to where it came out in the hay field. Fortunately, he noticed, they had continued to travel at a gallop through the hay, leaving a plain and easily followed trail behind.

He returned to Peabody. "All right, Len. You can go back now."

"Don't you want some help? I can have a dozen men here in two hours. That will still leave plenty of time to run down their trail before dark."

Gatewood said: "No help. I'd like to stop this feud where it is right now."

"They'll kill you. If they're desperate enough to kill Galt, they're desperate enough to kill you."

Gatewood said: "Thanks just the same."

"How's Lena?"

Gatewood looked at him in surprise and Peabody said lamely:

"I had a daughter her age. My Ruth even looked a little bit like her."

"Looked?"

"She died. Typhoid. Before I went to work for Galt."

"Lena lost her baby. Guy tried to force her to come back out here and she fell."

"I'm sorry. I really am. Lena's a real nice girl."

Gatewood didn't seem to know what to say. Peabody caught his horse, mounted, and rode away. Two hundred yards beyond he turned and raised a hand.

Gatewood mounted and took up the killers' trail. He knew who they were. He knew where they were going. But he had to follow trail because he needed proof.

The trail went straight across the hay field and climbed the ridge. Straight as an arrow it headed for the Dymond place.

Gatewood was able to follow it at a trot. Occasionally he raised his glance and looked ahead, more as a habitual precaution than because he feared they'd ambush him. They were too scared to think of anything, even of hiding the trail they made. They hadn't planned anything beyond just getting home.

XIII

The sun was low in the western sky when Gatewood came over the last ridge. He halted and stared down into the narrow valley at the haphazardly scattered buildings of the Dymond Ranch.

All the way here, he had tried to plan what he would do when he arrived, how he would capture the two who had killed Galt Majors. He had reached no conclusions, and had finally decided he would simply have to do what seemed best at the time.

No smoke rose from the chimney of the house. The chickens were heading for the chicken house, preparatory to roosting for the night. No horses were in the corral. The place looked deserted.

Gatewood started down the ridge. He knew he was close enough to be hit by a rifle bullet fired from the house, so he watched it intently, for movement in the windows, for the blossoming of smoke from the muzzle of a gun. Nothing happened. Nothing moved. Made nervous by this strange lack of activity, he suddenly dug spurs into his horse's sides.

The animal broke into a hard gallop. Gatewood kept his eye on the house, and swerved in behind the barn as soon as possible. He reached the shelter of the barn without being shot at, and left his horse precipitately, yanking the rifle out of the saddle boot as he did.

Against the barn wall, he paused, letting his breathing grow regular and quiet again. He was scared and he didn't mind admitting it. The Dymond brothers were dangerous. Having killed, they wouldn't hesitate to kill again. The fact that he was sheriff wouldn't mean a thing.

Nothing happened. He heard no sound but that of the breeze sighing past the tall barn gable above his head. He eased to the corner from where he could see the house. He could detect no sign of life.

They must have left, he told himself. They had probably gone to town, either to see their father or to break him out of jail. But he still took no chances. Leaving the corner of the barn, he sprinted toward the house, zigzagging as he ran to throw off any hidden gunman's aim.

He reached it without incident. Still wary, however, he edged along the outside wall to the door. Bracing himself, holding the rifle in his right hand, finger curled over the trigger, he opened the kitchen door with his left. He didn't hesitate once it was open but leaped inside, instantly jumping sideways, putting his back to the wall.

No one was in the kitchen. Relaxing slightly now, he moved on through it into the other rooms beyond. They, also, were empty.

Quickly he went back outside. He peered into the barn but saw no one there. He went around it to where his horse stood, reins trailing on the ground. Mounting, he backtracked up the ridge until he picked up the trail of the two horsemen he had been following. He continued to follow trail from here and it led him straight to the kitchen door.

He had something now that he could swear to in court, even if he didn't know which two of the four Dymond brothers he had been following.

He turned his horse and headed down the road toward town. Finding the Dymond place deserted was a let-down. But he knew the showdown with the Dymond brothers had only been postponed. If they were in town, they would be trying to break their father out of jail. It was up to him to get there in time to stop them if he could.

Clem and Ross pulled their plunging horses to a halt at the Dymonds' kitchen door in midafternoon. Both horses were lathered and blowing hard. Both men were as out of breath as if they had been running, too.

Clem swung to the ground. He turned his head toward Ross. "Get fresh horses and turn these loose."

Ross took the reins of his brother's horse and rode toward the corral. Clem went into the house.

Nate and Leon were both in the kitchen. The empty whiskey bottle stood on the table. Neither man was drunk, but plainly both had headaches judging from the way they squinted and winced when the door opened and the sunlight brightened the inside of the room.

Nate squinted at Clem and asked: "What are you doin' back

so soon? Didn't you see Galt?"

Clem said: "We saw him. Ross shot him and he's dead."

"Shot him? Why, for Christ's sake? Did he try and shoot you?"

Clem shook his head. "Ross got excited when Galt tried to get away."

"You're sure Galt was dead?"

"Hell, yes, I'm sure," Clem said irritably. "I know when a man's dead."

"How? You ain't seen so many dead men."

"I looked at his chest. He wasn't breathin'. He was dead, I tell you. I know he was."

Nate said: "Oh God! We're really in trouble now."

"We got to get Pa out of jail. He'll tell us what to do."

"More likely he'll kick the hell out of you an' Ross." A frown touched Nate's forehead. "I suppose you came right home. I suppose you left a trail."

Clem nodded sheepishly. "We wasn't thinkin' very good. We was scared. You'd've done the same damn' thing."

Leon nodded grudgingly. "I guess we would." He got to his feet. "Come on. We'd better get to town. Maybe Pa can think of somethin' we can do."

"What about Gatewood? What if we run into him?"

"If we run into him, then we'll know he don't know Galt is dead. Where'd you leave Galt, anyway?"

"Three or four miles south of the house."

"An' what about his horse?"

"He's loose."

"Then he'll go home, but maybe not right away. Maybe they ain't even found the body yet."

All three went out into the bright sunlight. Ross was approaching from the corral with two horses. He gave the reins of one to Clem. Nate and Leon hurried to the corral for their own horses. The two that Ross had just turned loose rolled in front of the corral, then got up, and trotted away.

Ordinarily they kept only a couple of horses in the corral at any time. If they needed more, they rode out and brought in the bunch. This morning, however, at dawn, Leon had driven in the bunch and had turned out the tired horse he had ridden from the Majors place last night. His head had been aching so that he hadn't bothered to turn all but two of the others out. He did so now, leaving the corral empty, its gate sagging open. He and Nate mounted and joined Clem and Ross. The four rode out toward town, holding their horses to a steady trot.

There was little talk. Once Ross asked: "How we goin' to get Pa out of jail?"

"Easy enough, if Gatewood's gone. We just walk in and unlock his cell."

"What if Gatewood's locked the door of the jail?"

"A bullet will bust the lock. Or a crowbar will rip off the hasp."

After that, there was silence once again. All four of the brothers were scared. They were scared over the consequences of what Ross had done. They were scared of what their father was going to do. But they were willing to accept whatever punishment he inflicted because they knew he would stand by them. He would tell them what to do.

They reached town in late afternoon. The streets were quiet. Several dogs lay sleeping in the buildings' shade. The loafers had disappeared from the hotel verandah, which was bathed by the rays of the afternoon sun.

They rode straight to the jail. Before they had dismounted, they could see that the door was locked. Clem said: "A crowbar'll be quieter. One of you go around to side window and talk to Pa. I'll go down to the blacksmith shop and borrow a crowbar."

He rode down the street toward the blacksmith shop, next to the livery barn. He was back out in less than a minute, a crowbar in his hand. He mounted and rode back to the jail.

The padlock hasp on the jail door surrendered almost immediately. The three, and Leon, who had been talking to Guy through the barred side window, went inside. The keys lay on Gatewood's desk. Clem unlocked the cell and let his father out.

Guy scowled at Ross. "You stupid fool!"

"He wouldn't listen. He tried to get away," Ross said sullenly.

"All right. It's done."

Clem had the sudden, strange feeling that his father was not really displeased. He asked: "What are we goin' to do? Gatewood will follow our trail straight home. He'll know it was one of us even if he don't know which one."

"Knowin' an' provin' are two different things. Come on. I want to know if old Galt had a will. And I want to know what it says."

He led out the door. A couple of townspeople stared briefly, then nervously glanced away and hurried on. The five crossed the street to a two-story building that housed the abstract office on the lower floor, the office of Ralph McCurtin, the town's lawyer, on the second floor. Guy said—"Stay here."—and climbed the outside stairway. He went in.

McCurtin's office was the one that faced the street. The other was vacant. Guy opened the door and stepped inside.

McCurtin was a middle-aged man with graying hair and a short, trimmed beard. He glanced up. "Hello, Guy, I thought Gatewood had you in jail."

"He did. I got out."

"You mean you broke out?"

"You could put it that way."

McCurtin glanced out the window worriedly. The jail door stood open. He asked: "Where's the sheriff?"

Guy shrugged. "I haven't any idea."

"What do you want from me?"

"I want to know about Galt Majors's will. Lena's part of the Majors family now and I got a right."

McCurtin shook his head. "I can't divulge that information. You know that."

Guy said: "You'd better divulge it, by God, if you know what's good for you."

"Are you threatening me?"

"You're damned right I am."

McCurtin said: "Don't make things worse than they already are. Galt might drop charges against you for shooting up his place last night."

Guy said: "The will. I don't want to hurt you, but I will."

McCurtin stubbornly shook his head.

Guy approached his desk. McCurtin got up and backed toward the window. Guy towered over him.

McCurtin sagged. "All right. All right. Maybe with Lena being part of the family and all, you *have* got a right."

"Now you're makin' sense."

McCurtin asked: "What do you want to know?"

"What happens to Galt's property if he was to die."

"It goes to his sons equally."

"And what if one of his sons is dead?"

"Then it goes to that son's issue."

"What's 'issue' mean?"

"Children."

Guy thought of the aborted child. He asked: "And what if there ain't no kids?"

"Then it goes to that son's wife, if he has one. If he doesn't, his share is to be divided equally among his brothers."

"You seem to know all this pretty well."

McCurtin shrugged faintly. "It's the most important will I've ever drawn. I could quote it word for word."

Guy nodded. "All right." He turned and tramped out. He went out on the landing and descended the stairs. He hadn't laid a hand on McCurtin and he wasn't worried about any complaint McCurtin might make to the sheriff after he was gone.

His sons looked questioningly at him. He said: "Let's get out of town."

They mounted and rode out of town, taking the road that went to the Dymond Ranch. Clear of the town, Guy halted his horse in the middle of the road. Clem asked: "Pa, what are we goin' to do?"

Guy said: "We ain't got nothin' an' the Majors family has got all the money in the world. Unless we do somethin', Ross is goin' to hang."

Ross's face turned a peculiar shade of green.

Guy said: "If we had money, we could put up some kind of fight."

"How we goin' to get it, Pa?"

"If Pres was dead, Lena would own a quarter of that whole damn' ranch. She wouldn't say no to helpin' her brother stay off the gallows, would she?"

All four of his sons shook their heads.

"Then scatter out and find that god-damn' Pres. I want him dead, but I want it to look like an accident. Understand?"

Hope showed in the eyes of his four sons. Hope where hope had previously disappeared. Ross said: "Pa, you just tell us where to go."

XIV

While Robert had stopped at the jail to tell Gatewood their father was missing, Pres had gone on to Doc Simms's house. He was still angry at his father for humiliating him, particularly for doing so in front of Lena. He told himself sourly that he didn't give a damn what had happened to the old son-of-a-bitch.

He knocked on the door, and, when Doc Simms answered it, he said: "Peabody found Pa's horse wanderin' loose a couple of miles from the house. The sheriff's goin' out and Peabody thinks you ought to come out, too."

"Does Peabody think he's hurt?"

Pres said sarcastically: "It kind of looks that way, doesn't it?"

"I can get along without your sarcasm, young man. You can tell Peabody I'll be right out."

Pres turned to go, but Doc called him back. "I don't know whether you care or not, but your wife lost her child last night. She's down in Gatewood's house, in case you're interested."

Pres swung around. "Why the hell should I be interested? She ain't goin' to be my wife for very long."

Doc slammed the door angrily. Pres stood scowling on the porch for a minute or two, hesitating about what he should do next. He didn't want to go back home. There would be nothing but confusion out there with everybody carrying on about the old man being gone and acting like they cared what might have happened to him.

It wouldn't hurt to have a couple of drinks before returning, he thought. He'd done what he was supposed to do. He had sent out Doc Simms and Robert had told Gatewood to go. There was nothing further he could do, and he sure as hell wouldn't be missed. By anyone.

He stepped down off Doc's porch, mounted, and headed for the saloon.

Dutch Hoffman was behind the bar. Pres said: "Whiskey, Dutch."

Dutch shoved a bottle and glass toward him. His eyes were cold and unfriendly, and suddenly that angered Pres. He said:

"What the hell are you lookin' at?"

"Nothin'," Dutch said pointedly, and turned away.

Pres gulped his drink. He growled: "Everybody in this whole damn' town blames me for what's happened to Lena. But it ain't my fault."

"Ain't it?"

"No, it ain't. Man gets tired of goin' out to Lily's place an' waitin' in line for his turn."

Dutch didn't say anything. Pres said: "One thing about Lily, though, that I can't say for some other people in this town. She don't hold herself out to be so damn' much better than everybody else."

"Why don't you go out and see her, then?"

Pres gulped his second drink. "Maybe, by God, I will." He grabbed the bottle and put the cork in it. "How much?"

"Seventy-five cents."

Pres threw a dollar on the bar. Carrying the bottle by its neck, he went outside. He mounted and turned downstreet toward the narrow road that led out to Lily Donovan's shack, a mile and a half from town. At the edge of town, he uncorked the bottle and took a drink. A little farther on, he took another one. He began to think of Lily and he kicked his horse's sides with his heels.

Guy sent Leon and Ross to the saloon to ask Dutch if he had seen Pres. He sent Clem to Gatewood's house, to see if Pres had been there. He and Nate positioned themselves on a ridge overlooking the road to the Majors Ranch, in case Pres should either be coming to town or returning to the ranch from it.

Now, in late afternoon, the saloon was beginning to fill. Ross and Leon went to the bar and ordered beer. Dutch brought them two foaming schooners and said: "Sorry about Lena. She's a real fine girl."

Both Leon and Ross nodded agreement. Dutch started away and Leon asked: "You seen Pres today? Lena was askin' where he was." It was a lie but Dutch wouldn't have any way of knowing that.

Dutch said: "Sure. He was in here about the middle of the afternoon."

"Where'd he go? You know?"

Dutch seemed hesitant to say. Leon said: "You do know, don't you?"

Dutch nodded reluctantly. "I know but it ain't goin' to help the way Lena feels if I tell."

Leon said: "We won't tell Lena. Not if we don't think she ought to know."

Dutch still seemed reluctant but at last he said: "Oh, hell, why should I protect him? He went out to Lily's place."

"Lily's place?" Leon scowled. "Why that son-of-a-bitch!"

Dutch said: "Don't tell Lena now. It would only hurt her and there ain't no use in that."

"We won't, Dutch. And thanks."

"What are you goin' to do?"

Leon said: "Nothin' serious. Punch him in the mouth is all."

"Wouldn't hurt my feelings none if you did," Dutch said, and went on to another customer.

Leon looked at Ross. "Well, it looks like it's up to us."

Ross gulped his beer and wiped his mouth with the back of his hand. "Let's go."

The two went out. They untied their horses, mounted, and rode out of town, heading for the narrow two-track road that led to Lily's shack.

The tracks of Pres's horse were plain in it, going toward it but not coming back. Pres could, of course, have cut straight across country after leaving Lily's place, and, if he'd left, they'd have to trail him. But there was a good chance he was still at

Lily Donovan's.

Half a mile short of the place, they left the road. Lily's house was in a brushy draw, in the bottom of which a tiny trickle of water ran. Ross and Leon approached cautiously through the brush, coming upon it from the rear so as to reduce the likelihood of their being seen. From a quarter mile away they could see Pres's horse through the heavy brush, still tied in front of Lily's shack.

The shack was built of railroad ties and had, in the early days, been used as a line shack by the Majors Ranch. Lily hadn't bought it. She'd just moved in. And nobody had ever tried to put her out, although the town ladies talked about evicting her often enough.

Leon said: "I'll ride around in front. I'll tell him Lena is asking for him, that she's dyin' and askin' for him. We'll get him out of there, and then maybe we can figure out something that will look like an accident."

Ross nodded.

Leon said: "You just wait back here in case anything goes wrong."

"All right."

Leon left the brushy draw and returned to the narrow road. He approached the shack along the road, openly, as if he was coming just now from town. He kicked his horse into a gallop so as to give his errand a sense of urgency.

Pulling up in front of the shack, he yelled: "Pres? Hey, Pres!"

For several moments there was only silence. He could detect no movement in the windows of the house. Then the door opened a crack and Pres's voice came out. "What? What the hell do you want from me?"

"It's Lena, Pres. She's dyin'. She asked me to come out after you."

"How'd you know where I was?"

"Dutch told us. I mean me."

"You lyin' son-of-a-bitch. There ain't nothin' wrong with Lena. At least not that bad."

"You'd better come on out or we'll come in after you. Lena wants you and you're comin' whether you like it or not." There was a real urgency about this, and Leon didn't like wasting time in argument. He started to dismount from his horse, reaching for the rifle in the boot as he did.

Another rifle roared from the crack in the door, and powder smoke rolled halfway to Leon's horse. Leon jerked as though hit by a giant fist. He twisted half around and tumbled from his horse. His shoulder was one large numb area and he was stunned, the way he once had been after being kicked in the chest by a mule. He thought in surprise: *He shot me! Damn him, he really did!*

His horse, startled, took several steps away, then looked back at him. Leon was exposed here in the dust, but he had managed to fall with his rifle in his hand. Fortunately it was hidden behind his body. Or he thought it was.

He didn't dare look toward the house, nor did he dare to move. He knew that any movement would bring a second shot, one that would probably finish him. Scarcely daring to breathe, he wondered where Ross was and what he was going to do.

He didn't have long to wait. A rifle suddenly opened up on the house from the brush at one side of the shack. The first bullets shattered both windows and drove Pres back away from the door, not, however, before he had closed and bolted it.

Leon released a long, slow sigh of relief. At least he wasn't going to feel that fatal bullet smashing into him just yet. He turned his head, trying to see where Ross had positioned himself.

Ross fired three more shots, two of them taking out pieces of glass that still remained in the window frames, the third thudding into the closed and bolted door. Ross's voice came worriedly: "Leon, you all right?"

Leon answered softly: "I got it in the shoulder and I'm bleedin'. Can you get to me?"

"I don't see how I can. He'll start shootin' the minute I show myself."

"Then you keep shootin' into the house. Maybe I can get up and get my horse."

Ross fired two more shots at the house and Leon tried to rise, wincing with pain and swaying from weakness as he did. This hadn't turned out the way they'd planned it. It hadn't turned out that way at all.

XV

One of Ross's last two shots had hit Lily Donovan. Suddenly she began to scream hysterically. Pres's voice, muffled by the walls of the house but plain enough, yelled: "You dumb bastards, you've hit Lily!"

Everything suddenly was still. Leon made it to his knees before the waves of weakness and dizziness forced him to fall back. There was a good-size pool of blood on the ground where he had lain, and he knew if he did not get help soon he was going to bleed to death. He turned his head, looking for Ross, but the horizon tipped crazily and his head fell back. He called—"Ross!"—but the word came out so weakly it is doubtful if it carried more than a dozen feet.

Lily's hysterically screaming voice was strong enough, however. Piercing and shrill, it sent shivers along Leon's spine in spite of his weakness and desperation.

From the house came Pres's voice: "She's bleedin'! We gotta get her to the doc!"

A lassitude that was almost pleasant had come over Leon. His shoulder didn't hurt. It just felt numb. The sky tipped and

107

turned and he felt the way he sometimes did when he was drunk. Dimly, as though from far away, he heard the pounding of a horse's hoofs, gradually diminishing until it had faded away completely, leaving a silence outside the shack that was more frightening than the roar of gunshots had been.

Ross was gone. He had left him here in the dust to die. He had run away. The realization stirred resentful anger in Leon's mind. It brought back a painful awareness of where he was, of the danger he faced. Pres would be coming out, soon, to see if he were dead. Finding him alive, Pres would finish him off as matter-of-factly as if he had been a wounded deer.

Lily had stopped screaming. Now she was moaning, and this was more unnerving than her screaming had been. Leon heard the bolt on the door as Pres shoved it back. He heard the squeak of the hinges as the door was opened cautiously. He was facing away from the house and he wouldn't see Pres as he approached. He would have to depend entirely on his ears.

His hand gripped the rifle receiver more tightly. He wondered if there was a cartridge in the chamber. There must be, he thought. It would have been automatic for him to work the lever as he left his horse, but he knew he couldn't count on it. He'd been hit while he was still on his horse and he might not have jacked a cartridge into the chamber. He would have to do so before he dared count on the gun firing.

Listening, with every muscle tensed, he heard the scuff of Pres's boots as he approached. He didn't want to wait until Pres had a bead on him, until Pres's finger tightened on the trigger. That would be too late. Nor did he want to roll too soon, while Pres was still too far away to make his shot a certainty.

Tensed to roll, he heard Lily's lost and terrified scream: "Pres! Don't leave me! For God's sake, Pres!"

Instinctively he knew that this was the instant for him to act.

Pres would be momentarily distracted by Lily's scream. He might even have turned his head.

He rolled, the rifle in his left hand. With his right, and feeling the pain in his shoulder for the first time as an awful burning, he worked the lever and jacked a cartridge into the chamber.

Pres stood ten feet away from him, a revolver in his hand. The hammer was back and it had been pointed straight at him. Pres, in turning, had pulled the gun slightly to one side so that it was no longer lined up on him.

Pres's head jerked back around. Frantically he tried to bring the gun to bear, but it was too late. Leon's finger tightened on the trigger and the rifle roared. Powder smoke billowed from the muzzle, enveloping Pres just as his own gun fired. The bullet, fired too soon, showered Leon with dirt.

Pres, hit, staggered back, driven by the force of the soft-nosed rifle slug. He struck the wall of the house and was held there momentarily by his own momentum. Then he slowly slid down the wall to a sitting position at its base. Blood leaked through his shirt as a spreading stain, almost in the exact center of his chest. The gun, which had fallen when he was hit, now lay almost halfway between him and Leon.

Leon raised the rifle to finish him, but he hadn't the strength to jack in another cartridge and fire it. It sagged and Leon released it. His head fell back and he lay, staring at the sky, conscious but without the strength to move. Pres made no sound. Lily had stopped moaning and now was completely still. Leon thought hazily that she probably was dead.

With a bullet in the chest, Pres had no chance. And unless help came soon, Leon had no chance, either. His blood was running out and it wasn't going to stop.

He had often wondered what it would be like to die. Now he knew. It was going to be like slipping off to sleep. It wasn't going to be hard at all. He would go to sleep and would not awake.

He took one last look at the sky. The sun was down and the clouds flamed orange. He hadn't realized it was so late.

Lassitude came over him and he closed his eyes. The whole world seemed to reel. If he had to die, this was the way, he thought. He felt as if he was very, very drunk.

The sound of Lily Donovan's screaming had struck sudden terror into Ross Dymond's heart. He had killed Galt, feeling no more afterward than if Galt had been a coyote, a wolf, or deer. But a woman was different, and particularly when that woman was Lily Donovan. Like most of the single men who lived in and near Cottonwood Springs, Ross had visited Lily whenever he had the price. It made him feel sick to think that she was hurt.

He raked his horse repeatedly on the way to town, forcing the animal to run. Unthinking terror had controlled him at first. Now he suddenly realized that Leon would think he had been abandoned. He had been, but nobody else need know he had. Ross could get Doc Simms and send him out. He himself could get a wagon and go after Leon with it.

Nobody had to know that he had panicked and run away. Even Leon wouldn't think he had if he sent Doc Simms out right away. The truth of the matter was that Leon probably had a better chance to live this way than if he had stayed and kept trying to smoke Pres out.

The clouds had faded from their brilliant orange and were turning gray as he rode into town. Heading straight for Doc Simms's house, he passed right by the jail. A horse was tied to the rail out front. As he passed, Gatewood came to the jail door. "Hey!"

Ross turned his head, but he didn't stop. Gatewood drew his gun. He yelled: "Hold it! I want to talk to you!"

Ross didn't want to take a chance on being shot. He pulled

his horse to a plunging halt. Gatewood stepped out into the street and walked toward him without holstering his gun. He asked: "Where are you going in such a rush?"

Ross still seemed to hear Lily's screams. He said: "Leon is shot and so is Lily Donovan. I'm going after Doc."

"Where are they?"

"Out at Lily's shack."

"Who else is there?"

"Pres Majors."

Gatewood didn't waste time asking any more questions. He said: "You go down to the livery stable and get a wagon. Have Buck throw a load of straw in it. I'll get Doc and go on out. You follow me."

Ross nodded. He turned his horse and galloped toward the livery barn. Gatewood untied his horse, mounted, and galloped up the street toward Doc's. Doc had gotten back from the Majors Ranch a couple of hours earlier. There had been nothing he could do out there, and so he hadn't stayed.

Gatewood ran to Doc's door and pounded urgently on it. When Doc came, he said: "Lily Donovan and Leon Dymond have been shot. Is your buggy put away?"

Doc nodded. "I didn't figure I'd have to go out again."

Gatewood said: "Get your bag. I'll hitch it up."

He hurried around the house to the stable in back of it. He put the harness on Doc's buggy horse, led him out, and backed him between the buggy shafts. When he had finished, he climbed in and drove the buggy through the vacant lot to the front of the house, where Doc was waiting with his bag. Gatewood climbed down and Doc climbed up. Gatewood said—"I'll see you at Lily's shack."—and galloped away.

Now that he had time to think, he could feel an outraged anger growing in him. Galt was dead, murdered before he could draw a gun. Now Leon and Lily were shot, he didn't know how seriously, but one or both of them might also die. What angered him was the senselessness of it. None of it had solved anything nor proved anything.

He reached Lily's shack. Pulling his plunging horse to a halt, he could see the devastation there. Leon lay on his back, staring at the sky. He was conscious but he had obviously lost an awful lot of blood. The ground beneath him was soaked with it.

Pres sat against the outside wall of the shack, barely conscious, hit in the chest. The whole front of his shirt was soaked with blood.

There was nothing Gatewood could do for either of them, and he knew Doc would be along very soon. He stepped into the shack.

Lily lay on the floor, dressed only in a loose wrapper, which had fallen open in the front. There was a small, bluish hole in her abdomen, from which a small trickle of blood had run. Her abdomen was bluish and distended from internal bleeding. Her face was pale.

Gatewood knelt beside her, automatically pulling her wrapper closed to cover her. She was unconscious. Her breathing was shallow and slow and he knew that she was near to death.

There was nothing he could do for her, either. He got up and went back outside. Pres glanced up at him, his eyes dull with shock and pain. Gatewood asked: "What happened? Can you talk?"

"They yelled for me to come out." Gatewood had to lean closer so that he could hear. "They said they were comin' in, so I shot Leon from the door."

"And Ross opened up on you."

"Uhn-huh. That's when Lily got hit."

"How did you get shot?"

"After Ross left, I came out to see if Leon was dead. He rolled over and shot me."

"Why'd they come out here after you?"

"They said Lena wanted me."

Gatewood knew that was a lie. And since it was a lie, there could be only one reason why Ross and Leon had come after Pres. They had intended to murder him. Galt was dead, and, if Pres was also dead, Lena would inherit a fourth interest in the Majors Ranch. They would probably have tried to make it look like an accident if they'd been able to get Pres away from Lily's place. But Pres hadn't trusted them and this was the result.

He heard hoofs and the wheels of Doc's buggy and turned his head. Doc stopped his buggy horse and climbed quickly down. He looked at Leon first, then went to Pres. He paused there only a moment, then went inside. Coming out, he said: "Lily's dead."

There was nothing Gatewood could say. Lily had been a prostitute, but she'd been a pleasant woman and she'd never hurt anyone. He was sorry she was dead, sorry she'd had to die this way.

By-passing Pres, Doc went to Leon. He cut away his shirt and quickly went to work to stop the bleeding. Gatewood asked: "What about Pres?"

Doc looked up and shook his head. Gatewood understood that Doc was only trying to save what could be saved. He knew Pres was dying, that there was no hope for him.

Doc hadn't quite finished when Gatewood heard a wagon coming along the road. It was now almost dark and Doc was working swiftly, trying to get through while he still could see. Ross turned the wagon around and stopped it near to where Leon lay. Doc straightened. "That's all I can do until we get him back to town."

Gatewood said: "Come on, Ross, help me load them up."

Ross climbed down. Together, and carefully, they lifted Leon to the wagon bed, which was filled with straw. After that, they went to Pres, who was still conscious, and lifted him. They laid him in the middle, beside Leon. The two looked at each other with bleak hatred, and looked away.

Gatewood and Ross laid Lily's body in last. Pres turned his head and looked at her. Gatewood couldn't tell whether he knew that she was dead or not.

Ross climbed back up onto the wagon seat. He drove out, holding the horses to a walk. Doc followed in his buggy and Gatewood brought up the rear. It was now almost completely dark.

The lights of Cottonwood Springs winked ahead. One by one the stars came out. Gatewood wondered how many more would have to die before Guy Dymond was satisfied.

XVI

The wagon halted in front of Doc's house in Cottonwood Springs. Doc's buggy drew up immediately behind. Doc got down and walked to the wagon. Leon was conscious but very pale, and his face was twisted with pain. Doc said: "I'll give you something for that pain as soon as I get you inside." He groped for and found Pres Majors's wrist. There was no pulse.

Gatewood and Ross approached and Doc said: "Bring Leon into the house. Leave Pres here. He's dead."

Ross stood there for several moments, too shocked to move. Gatewood said impatiently: "Come on, dammit. Pick up his feet."

Numbly Ross did, and Gatewood carried his head and shoulders. They took Leon into the house and followed Doc into a bedroom, where they laid Leon on the bed. Gatewood went back out, tied his horse to the tailgate of the wagon, mounted to the seat, and drove away. Ross followed a little way behind, but before Gatewood reached the Mendenhall Furniture and Undertaking Company on Fifth Street, he had dropped back and disappeared. Arriving at Mendenhall's, Gatewood got down and tied the team. He noticed now that Ross was gone, but it didn't particularly worry him. He knew he could pick Ross up anytime.

There were no lights inside the store, so Gatewood untied his horse and rode to Mendenhall's house three blocks away. The undertaker agreed to open up and Gatewood returned to the store, where he waited until the man arrived. The two of them then carried the bodies inside and laid them on slabs in Mendenhall's back room, used for the undertaking side of the business. Mendenhall covered them with sheets and Gatewood left.

Once more tying his horse behind the wagon, he mounted the seat and drove it to the livery barn. After that, he walked back to the jail.

There was a light in his house and he wondered how Lena was. He tied his horse and went into the jail.

He wished he knew where Ross had gone, and where Guy was now. He wondered if they were through making trouble for tonight. He sure hoped so. He was tired. He wanted to get some supper and go to bed.

Ross Dymond followed the wagon for only a couple of blocks. Then he dropped back. He'd be a fool if he let Gatewood put him in jail. His father and Nate were waiting out on the road to the Majors place. They'd want to know what had happened. His father would probably give him hell because Pres's death hadn't been made to look like an accident. But he didn't see how he and Leon could have done anything differently. They hadn't counted on Pres cutting loose from inside the shack the way he had.

He left town, taking the road to the Majors Ranch. It was dark and he didn't know how he'd find his father and Nate and Clem. He'd just have to hope that they'd find him.

They did. They loomed up ahead of him in the road and Guy's voice came harshly: "Hold it right there."

Ross said: "Pa, it's me. It's Ross."

"Did you find him?"

"Yes, sir. We found him."

"Well?" Guy asked impatiently.

"Pa, he's dead. He. . . ."

"Good," Guy said approvingly. "Did you make it look like an accident?"

"That's what I got to tell you, Pa. It didn't turn out like we thought it ought to."

"What are you talkin' about?"

"He was out at Lily Donovan's. I stayed out of sight an' Leon rode up to the shack an' told him to come out. We figured once we got him outside, we could work out something that would look like an accident. Only he shot Leon instead of comin' out, and then I had to open up on the shack."

"Shot Leon? Is he . . . ?"

"He's at Doc's. He lost a lot of blood, but I think he's goin' to be all right."

"What happened then?"

Ross hesitated.

Guy said impatiently: "Well?"

"That whore . . . Lily . . . she caught a bullet. I didn't mean to hit her. I was just tryin' to keep Pres's head down so's I could get to Leon an' see how bad he was hurt."

"Oh, hell. How bad is *she* hurt?"

"She's dead."

"You stupid idiot."

"I couldn't help it, Pa. I could see Leon layin' there hurt. You'd 'a' done the same damn' thing!"

Guy was silent for a moment. Then he said, in a calmer voice: "Did you kill Pres, too?"

"No. I couldn't get near to Leon so I went to town for Gate-wood and the Doc. We brought a wagon back, an', when we got there, Pres was lyin' outside close to Leon. I guess he came out to see if Leon was dead an' Leon shot him."

Guy was silent for a long, long time. At last Clem said: "Pa, maybe it ain't so bad. Ross says Pres shot first, an' hit Leon. So the shootin' Ross done was self-defense, wasn't it? He was just tryin' to help Leon."

"You figure they'll call the woman's gettin' hit an accident?"

"Right."

Guy said: "Good enough. We won't worry about it any more. We got some settlin' up to do with the law, but we're in a hell of a sight better position that we was. Lena owns a quarter of the Majors Ranch, as of right now. What do you think of that?"

"How's she gonna get her hands on it?"

"That's what I've been thinkin' on. We're goin' back to town. We're goin' to get us a wagon an' put a featherbed in it. Then we're goin' to take Lena an' go out to the Majors place. We're gonna claim Lena's one-fourth interest. Once we're there, they'll play hell gettin' us out again."

"What about Gatewood?"

"We lock him up in his own damn' jail."

Clem said enthusiastically: "It'll work. I think it's really gonna work."

"Sure it's gonna work. Come on, let's go back to town. Clem, you and Nate take care of Gatewood. Ross, you get the wagon an' a featherbed. I'll keep a look-out for the Majors boys until you all get to Gatewood's house."

They reached the edge of Cottonwood Springs. Ross left the others and headed for the livery barn. Guy stayed with his remaining two sons until they reached Gatewood's house. Then he stopped, and they went on to the jail next door.

There was a light in it. The door sagged open slightly because

117

of the broken hasp and lock. Quietly they approached the door. Reaching it, Clem kicked it open, entering with his rifle in his hands, cocked and ready to fire.

Gatewood was caught in the act of rising from his desk. Clem said: "Easy, Sheriff. We don't mean you no harm. We just don't want you messin' in our business for an hour or so."

Gatewood was careful not to reach for his gun. He knew the Dymonds had their backs to the wall and he knew they were dangerous. Clem said: "Nate, get his gun."

Nate eased around in back of Gatewood and took his gun. Clem nodded at him and Nate raised it. He brought it down sharply against the top of Gatewood's head and the sheriff slumped.

Nate caught him before he hit the floor. He dragged him back into one of the cells and dumped him on the bunk. Clem brought some rope and they tied his hands and feet. They stuffed a gag into his mouth, tying it in place with strips torn from one of the blankets. Clem asked: "Where's the keys?"

"They were layin' on his desk."

"Get them."

Nate got the keys and they locked Gatewood's cell. Leaving, they blew out the lamp and closed the door. Clem whispered: "Everybody will just think that he's asleep."

Nate chuckled. "He is."

Guy was waiting next door for them. The three fidgeted impatiently until they heard the wagon coming. Ross halted it and called: "Pa, I don't know where to get a featherbed!"

"Never mind. We'll take the one out of Gatewood's house."

Ross halted the wagon and held the team while Guy, Clem, and Nate went up the walk to Gatewood's house. They entered without knocking. Mrs. Campbell turned her head and stared at them with startled fright. Guy said: "It's all right, Missus Campbell. We're just goin' to take Lena out where she belongs."

"Doctor Simms said she wasn't to be moved."

"Well, ma'am, we just talked to Doc Simms and he said it was goin' to be all right."

"I don't believe you. He wouldn't say a thing like that."

"Well he did, ma'am. If you don't believe it, you just go on up and ask him."

"While you take Lena. No, siree. I'm staying here. And you're not moving her."

Guy said softly: "Ma'am, we *are* movin' her. And you'll be better off if you don't interfere."

She crossed the room to the couch where Lena lay. Lena had just awakened, and the sleep was still in her eyes. Mrs. Campbell positioned herself in front of Lena. Guy said: "Clem, Gatewood ought to have some kind of mattress on his bed. Get it and throw it in the wagon."

Clem went into Gatewood's bedroom. A few minutes later he came out again, lugging a huge featherbed. He took it out the front door.

Guy said: "Ma'am, stand aside."

"No! You can't make me stand aside."

Guy swung his hand. The flat of it struck the side of Mrs. Campbell's face. She staggered to one side from the force of it, giving a small cry of surprise and pain. Lena said: "Pa, you keep your hands off her. I'll go with you, if that's what you want."

"It's what I want. You want I should carry you?"

Nate said: "I'll carry her, Pa." He crossed to the couch, slid his arms under Lena, and lifted her, blankets and all.

Mrs. Campbell shrilled: "You'll be sorry for this, you, you . . . !"

Guy didn't bother to look at her. He followed Nate out into the street. With considerable gentleness, Nate laid his sister in the back of the wagon on the featherbed. He sat on the tailgate. Guy, Ross, and Clem climbed to the seat. The wagon creaked away, the horses traveling at a walk.

The lights of the town dropped behind and disappeared. Once Nate asked softly—"You all right, Sis?"—and she replied sleepily: "I'm all right. Where are we going?"

"Out to the Majors place. Did you know that Galt and Pres are dead?"

It was a while before she replied. Then she said: "No. I didn't know. But a lot of things are beginning to make sense."

"You own a fourth of it. Did Pa tell you that?"

"No. He didn't tell me. But I figured it out. Who killed them? Pa?"

"Ross killed Galt. Leon killed Pres. But it was self-defense."

"Where is Leon?"

"He's at Doc's. Pres shot him before he got Pres."

"Is he hurt very bad?"

"Ross said he lost a lot of blood but that he's goin' to be all right."

She was silent then, and so was Nate. They rolled into the Majors yard before 11:00 P.M. Ross went into the house to light some lamps. Nate and Clem carried Lena in. Guy stood by the wagon, a shotgun in his hands, until Len Peabody and half a dozen of the crew came out of the bunkhouse to find out what was going on.

Guy said: "You all know that Galt is dead. Pres is dead, too. Lena's come to take possession of what is rightfully hers. I expect you men to defend this place in case it is attacked."

Peabody asked: "Who's goin' to attack it, for God's sake?"

"The rest of the Majors family. To try and put us out."

Peabody hesitated for a long time. At last one of the men asked: "What are we supposed to do, Peabody?"

"Hell, I don't know. I reckon Lena's got a right to be here with the old man dead, an' Pres dead, too. She owns a quarter of the place. On the other hand, I ain't goin' to fight old Galt's sons. So I just reckon I'll quit an' go to town. Mebbe when all this gets straightened out, I'll come back again."

He turned and walked toward the bunkhouse to pack his gear. The other hands followed him. Guy called: "Double wages for anybody that stays!"

Nobody answered him. Scowling, he turned and went into the house, slamming and bolting the door behind.

XVII

Galt Majors's three sons had never felt so lost or so inadequate. Galt was dead. The tough old patriarch, who had always told each of them exactly what to do, would do so no more. His body was in the back of the light spring wagon, covered with a blanket. There was a carpetbag in the wagon with him that contained his best Sunday suit, a change of underwear, a tie, and a clean white shirt.

They reached town just before 6:00 P.M. and drove straight to the undertaker's. Donald went in, while the other two waited uncomfortably beside the wagon.

Mendenhall came out, carrying a stretcher. He laid it in the wagon bed beside Galt's body, and then he and his assistant carefully lifted the body onto it. Afterward they lifted the stretcher and carried it inside.

Donald followed, carrying the carpetbag. The other two remained outside. Donald said: "I don't know when to tell you to have the funeral. I suppose we ought to allow enough time for people to find out. There'll have to be something in the newspaper and that won't come out until tomorrow."

Mendenhall said: "This is Wednesday. How about Saturday? Around two o'clock?"

"I guess that will be all right."

"At the Methodist Church?"

Donald nodded. "I'll speak to the preacher. Pa never went, but he paid in enough."

"Fine. I'll take care of everything else . . . the obituary, the casket, the burial plot."

Donald said: "He'd want to be buried at the ranch. That's where my mother is."

"Of course."

"Is that all, then?"

Mendenhall nodded. "Come in on Saturday morning."

Donald hadn't known it would be so simple. He'd supposed there would be any number of details that had to be arranged. Feeling lost, he went outside again. His brother James looked at him and asked: "What now?"

"That's all."

"That's all?"

Donald smiled ruefully. "Seems funny, doesn't it, that a man who accumulated so much in the world can't take any of it out with him? Just his black Sunday suit, a clean shirt, a tie, and some clean underwear."

"I need a drink," James said.

"All right. Let's go to the hotel." The three climbed to the wagon seat and Donald drove to the hotel.

The bar in the hotel was a little more elegant than was the saloon and the Majors brothers usually did their drinking there. The place was dark and cool, furnished with heavy, dark mahogany furniture. The bar was also of mahogany, and ornately carved, as was the frame around the backbar mirror. The bartender was a Negro named Sam Washington. He was completely bald and wore a white shirt and a white apron. He said: "I'm sorry about Mistuh Majors. He was a fine gentleman."

Donald thought: *He was like hell. He was tough and strong but he was no gentleman.* He kept the thought to himself and said:

"Whiskey, Sam."

"Yes, suh." Sam put a bottle and three glasses out. Donald poured three drinks and raised his glass. He almost made a toast and then decided against it. James asked: "What are we going to do?"

"About the ranch? Go right on with it, I guess. Peabody can keep it running the same as he always has. I can take care of the ranch accounts just like I always have. You two and Pres can sit on your butts just like you always have."

Neither James nor Robert seemed to resent what he had said. James grinned and said: "Won't seem the same without the old man giving us hell all the time."

Donald downed his drink and poured himself another one. He downed that one quickly and poured a third.

Outside, the sun was down. Sam Washington went around lighting all the lamps. Donald felt as if a great weight had been lifted from his back. He felt free for the first time in his life. He felt an exhilaration that had nothing to do with the whiskey he had drunk.

The old man had been a tyrant. He'd never given his sons any responsibility. He'd never let them have an idea of their own. He'd never let them have anything and he hadn't paid them any salary.

But now everything he had accumulated belonged to the four of them. Donald knew almost exactly what the ranch was worth. He knew how many cattle there were. He knew how much money was in the bank.

All told, the ranch was worth $750,000. That meant each one of them had more than $175,000 of his own. The sum was staggering. Donald himself had never had more than $100 of his own at any given time. Neither had his brothers. Now they could have anything they wanted. They could travel. They could get married. They could go some place else and have a ranch of their own, if they didn't want to stay. Nothing was impossible.

The thought was more intoxicating than the whiskey. Donald looked at his brothers. He could see that their thoughts were similar to his own. James asked: "What are *you* going to do?"

Donald grinned. "Damned if I know. I'm going to have to think on it."

James looked at Robert. "What are you going to do?"

"Maybe, just for the hell of it, I'll have a crack at running that big ranch."

James said: "I'm going to get me the biggest featherbed I can find. Then I'm going to get me fifteen whores and go to bed with all of them at once."

Donald said wryly: "You must take after the old man. That's what he'd have wanted when he was your age if all the stories I've heard are true."

The three left the bar and went to a table. They ordered supper. By the time it arrived, it was completely dark outside. By the time they had finished eating it, it was after 9:00 P.M.

Mendenhall, the undertaker, came in. He crossed the room to the table where the three brothers were. He said: "Have you heard about Pres?"

Donald shook his head. "What about him?"

"He's dead."

"Dead? What do you mean, he's dead? He was all right this afternoon."

"I'm sorry. He's down at my place now. Along with Lily Donovan."

"Lily Donovan? What happened to them?"

Mendenhall said: "Mind if I sit down?"

Donald pushed a chair toward him and the undertaker sat down. He said: "Pres was out at Lily's place. Ross and Leon Dymond found him there. They challenged him to come out and Pres shot Leon through a crack in the door. Ross opened up on the shack and Lily was hit. Ross came to town for Doc, and, while he was gone, Pres came out to see if Leon was dead. Leon raised up and shot him in the chest."

"Where's Leon now?"

"He's at Doc's. He's lost a lot of blood. He nearly died himself, I guess."

Donald waved to Sam to bring another glass. He poured Mendenhall a drink. The undertaker gulped it and got to his feet. "I saw your wagon outside and I thought you'd want to know."

Donald nodded his thanks. Mendenhall went out.

All three of the brothers were surprised and shocked. But not so much that they couldn't think. Donald said: "You know what this means, don't you?"

"That Pres's share of the ranch goes to Lena Dymond?"

Donald nodded. "And if I know Guy, he's already thinking of claiming it."

James said: "We'd better go down and see Gatewood."

All three brothers got to their feet. Their drinks and meals would go on the ranch account with the hotel. They hurried out into the night.

The jail was dark. So was Gatewood's house. Knowing Lena had been staying at Gatewood's house, Donald supposed that Gatewood was sleeping at the jail and that he had already gone to bed. He halted the wagon in front and climbed down. He pounded on the jail door, startled when it swung open as he did. He called: "Sheriff? You there?"

There was no answer, but there was a muffled sound from inside the jail. Donald went in, feeling a kind of chill running along his spine. Once more he called—"Sheriff?"—while he fumbled in his pocket for a match.

Finding one, he struck it and looked for the lamp.

There was one on the desk and he lit it. The jail office was empty. Donald glanced toward the cells at the rear.

Once more he heard that muffled sound. He said—"Someone's back there."—and picked up the lamp. He went back and saw Gatewood trussed up like a pig on the bunk in one of the cells.

He asked: "What happened to you?"

The sheriff made a muffled, unintelligible sound. James said: "He's gagged. He can't talk."

"See if you can find the keys."

Once more Gatewood made a muffled sound. He sounded angry and Donald said defensively: "We can't do a damn' thing about that gag until we find the keys."

James had lit another lamp in the office. He was looking around for the keys.

Gatewood began to struggle on the bunk. He put his face down and wriggled violently, obviously trying to loosen the gag. He kept trying until he had succeeded in loosening it enough to speak. "Extra set in the bottom left-hand drawer of the desk. 'Way in the back."

James found them and brought them to Donald. Donald made no move to unlock the cell. James said: "Ain't you going to let him out?"

"I don't know. What happened, Sherm? How'd you get locked in?"

"Clem and Nate Dymond came busting in here a while ago and put a gun on me. They knocked me out, tied me, and locked me up in here."

Donald said: "You two stay here. I'm going next door and see if Lena is still there."

He hurried next door to Gatewood's house. He knocked on the door. There was no reply. He knocked again, louder and more persistently. Still there was no answer to his knock.

He tried the door and found it unlocked. He opened it and

went inside. He struck a match, found the lamp, and lit it. Obviously Lena had been on the couch, because a pillow and blanket were lying there. But Lena was gone.

Donald went into the bedroom, carrying the lamp. It was empty, but one thing caught his attention immediately. The mattress was missing from the bed.

He returned to the living room and blew out the lamp. He went out and closed the door. He knew where Lena was. She was out at the ranch. With Guy Dymond. With Clem and Nate and Ross. They were staking a claim to a fourth interest in the ranch and they figured possession was nine points of the law.

He returned to the jail. He said: "Lena's gone. So is the mattress from the sheriff's bed."

"What are we going to do?"

Donald had never faced a decision like this before. He was surprised to realize that it wasn't as difficult as he had expected it to be. There must be something of the old man in him, he thought. He must have inherited some of the old man's toughness and it had just taken trouble to bring it out.

He said: "We're going to run the sons-of-bitches off."

"Just the three of us?"

"I figure Peabody and the crew will be along before very long. If they don't show up by the time we're ready to go, we'll probably meet them on the road. Peabody don't like Guy Dymond any better than we do and he won't work for him."

"I wish we could be sure of that."

"We can be sure of it. Come on, let's go. We need horses. There are plenty of guns right here."

From the cell in back, Gatewood yelled: "Let me loose!"

James walked back and looked into the cell. "We didn't put you there, and we ain't going to get you out. We'll just kill our own snakes if you don't mind." He went to the gun rack and got guns for his brothers and for himself.

He followed his brothers out into the night, leaving the jail and sheriff's office dark. The three hurried toward the livery barn.

XVIII

For a full minute after the Majors brothers had left, Gatewood was too furious to do anything. Then, violently, he began to fight his bonds. Savagely and bitterly he cursed Guy Dymond and his sons, and when he was through with them cursed Galt Majors's sons with equal bitterness.

Next he opened his mouth and began to yell. It was late but his shouts might be heard. Someone might hear and come in and let him out. He didn't know what Donald Majors had done with the keys. If he'd taken them with him, then the cell door would have to be forced or the bars would have to be cut.

Growing hoarse, he stopped yelling momentarily. He listened, but he heard no sound. He began to yell again, less frantically because he realized that his voice would have to hold out until he made somebody hear.

Pausing, he listened once again. Still he heard no sound. He wondered what time it was. 10:00 or 11:00, he supposed. Most of the townspeople were at home in bed. Only drunks would be on the street and he'd have to be lucky to make one of them hear. But if he didn't make someone hear, he'd be here all night.

He was worried about Lena. Doc had said she wasn't to be moved, under any circumstances. Yet Guy had taken her, apparently making only a feeble effort to cushion her from the wagon's jolting by putting a mattress in the back of it. There was no assurance, however, that the cushioning would be enough. She might need Doc desperately before the night was out.

He began to struggle again against the ropes that tied his

hands and feet. It was no use. The ropes were too tight and he had been tied too long. By now, the circulation and been cut. His hands and feet were swollen and partly numb.

He began to yell again. Three times he would yell as loud as he could. Then he would stop to listen, then yell three more times. Finally he heard the scuffing of feet in the street in front of the jail.

He forgot the need to keep his voice from giving out. He forgot everything but the moment's desperate urgency. He yelled at the top of his lungs, first facing toward the outside door, then facing toward the open window of the cell.

Hoarse, he stopped. He heard the door squeak and heard a voice: "Sheriff?"

"In here! Light a lamp and see if you can find the keys! I'm locked in one of the cells!"

Someone came into the office. A match flared, and a moment later a lamp came to life. Gatewood said: "Hurry! See if the keys are on my desk." He couldn't see who it was yet, but when the man turned toward the desk, he recognized him. It was Ernie Mead, on his way to help close up the saloon.

Ernie fumbled around on the desk for a long time. Impatiently Gatewood said: "Can't you find them?"

"They ain't here, Sheriff."

"Then look around the office. They've got to be there some place."

Ernie picked up the lamp and moved around the office. "Ain't here," he said.

"All right. Go find Melvin Hill. Get him out of bed if you have to. Tell him to bring whatever he's going to need to cut me out of here."

Ernie grunted assent and hurried out the door. He left the lamp burning on the desk.

He was gone for what seemed to Gatewood like an hour.

129

When he returned, Melvin Hill, the town blacksmith, was with him. Hill had stuffed his nightshirt into his trousers. He was carrying a hacksaw and a sledge. He looked through the bars at Gatewood. "What happened? Who did that to you?"

"Guy Dymond. Hurry up. Get me out of here."

"Sure." Hill went to work on one of the bars, sawing it close to the floor. The saw rasped back and forth, back and forth, interminably. Gatewood had trouble curbing his impatience even though he knew Hill was working as swiftly as he could.

The saw went through at last. Hill stood up and hit the bar several times with the sledge. It didn't give, so he gripped it with both hands and bent it to one side. He squeezed through, crossed the cell to the cot, and with his pocket knife cut Gatewood's bonds.

Gatewood sat up on the edge of the cot. He got carefully to his feet, took a step toward the door, and fell flat on his face. Hill helped him up and back to the cot, where he sat down again, muttering angry curses beneath his breath. He rubbed his numb wrists for several moments, then bent over and rubbed his ankles and his feet. When he stood up the second time, Hill steadied him. Gatewood hobbled to the gap in the bars and squeezed through.

Hill asked: "You gettin' up a posse, Sherm?"

Gatewood hesitated. He had a hunch he was going to be heading into a full-scale war. Guy Dymond and three of his sons were holed up in the Majors house. The three Majors brothers, along with Len Peabody and most of the crew, were undoubtedly going to try to drive them out. It would take a good-size posse to cope with a situation like that.

He opened his mouth to tell Hill to help him round a posse up, then closed it again. Lena was in that house and bullets would rip through the thin frame walls as if they weren't there. What had happened to Lily Donovan could happen to Lena.

And no matter how big a posse he took out there, Guy Dymond wouldn't come out. Not until he was carried out.

He said: "No posse. I can take care of it."

"You know where Guy Dymond is?"

"I know."

He went to the gun rack and got a double-barreled shotgun. He got two hands full of shells from the desk drawer and stuffed them into his pockets. There still was no strength in his hands and his ankles threatened to give out on him, but he knew that by the time he got out to the Majors place they would probably feel almost normal again.

He picked up his revolver from the office floor, blew out the lamp, and followed Ernie Mead and Hill out the door. He said: "Thanks, Ernie. Thanks, Mel."

"You're welcome, Sherm."

Gatewood headed for the livery barn. His head ached from the blow that Nate had struck him earlier with the barrel of his gun. His feet and hands hurt as the circulation of blood through them improved.

Buck, the stableman, had gone home for the night, but the stable doors were never locked. Gatewood swung them back and went inside. He saddled, led his horse outside, closed the stable doors, then mounted him. He kicked him in the sides and pointed him down the street. As soon as he was out of town, he kicked the horse again, forcing him to gallop.

Nothing like this had ever happened before. Not in all the time he'd been sheriff here. Now, in two days' time, three people had been killed senselessly.

And more people were going to be killed if he didn't put a stop to it.

The three Majors brothers met Len Peabody and the crew halfway to the ranch. They milled around in the road while

Donald and Len Peabody talked. Donald's first question was: "How come you let the bastards in the house?"

Peabody said: "Hell, Mister Majors, they were in the house before we knew what was goin' on. It was pretty late when they got there and we were all asleep."

"What did Guy say?"

"Said Lena owned a quarter interest in the place now that Pres was dead. When he found out we were leavin', he offered double wages to anybody that stayed and worked for him."

"All right. Let's go take the place back from him."

"What about the sheriff? Hadn't we ought to leave it up to him?"

"He's out of it. Guy tied his hands and feet and gagged him and locked him in a cell."

"And you didn't let him out?"

Donald said: "Guy Dymond and his sons are responsible for Pa's death and for Pres's. Gatewood had Guy in jail once and he got out. If we leave it up to him, he'll just put Guy in jail again. And he'll probably get out again. I don't know how the rest of you feel about it, but I'm not going to feel safe until Guy is dead. I say this is our chance to get rid of him for good. We'd be fools if we don't take it."

Peabody hesitated. Donald asked: "How do you others feel?"

James said: "I think you're right. We'll never have a better chance. I say let's go out there and get rid of them once and for all."

Donald looked at Robert. "How about you?"

"Sure." Robert chuckled. "I just wish the old man could see us now."

Donald looked at Peabody. The foreman's face was only a blur in the darkness and he couldn't see what Peabody's expression was. He said: "They're trespassing. They've seized our property. They've got no rights out there. They murdered Pa and they murdered Pres. No court in the country would say that gave them a right to a quarter of the ranch."

Peabody said: "All right." He turned and looked at the crew men clustered in the road. "I'm going, but that don't mean you have to go. I guess it's up to each of you to decide it for himself."

Donald said: "A hundred dollars extra to every man if we clean that bunch out of there before the sheriff can interfere."

There was no hesitation after that. Excitedly the men followed as Robert, James, and Donald led them toward the ranch.

At the gate, Donald said: "Surround the place. We'll give them a chance to surrender before we cut loose on them."

He waited while Peabody assigned each man a place. The men dispersed, disappearing into the darkness immediately.

Donald, James, and Robert stayed with Peabody. The four rode down the lane, dismounting while they were still two hundred yards away. They crept closer on foot, staying in shadows, knowing Guy would kill them if he could.

Donald got to within a hundred feet of the house. Standing behind a tree, he yelled: "Guy?"

The voice came from an upstairs window of the house. "I'm here."

Donald yelled: "You've got a choice! You can give up and there'll be no shooting. Or you can do it the hard way and make us dig you out. We've got Peabody and the whole damned crew. You're surrounded and you haven't got a chance."

Guy yelled: "You'll let us go?"

"I said I would."

"You're a liar. The minute we come out, you'll cut us down."

"That's a chance you'll just have to take."

Guy yelled back: "We got a right here an' we're goin' to stay. Lena owns a fourth of this an' we're Lena's family."

"Then you won't come out?"

"Nope. Come on in an' get us out. If you can."

Donald bawled: "All right! Open up on them!"

Immediately a fusillade crackled from all around the house. Glass tinkled as the windows shattered. Bullets thudded into the walls of the house, in most cases tearing through. One or two ricocheted, whining away eerily into the night.

The fusillade died, and immediately guns opened up from the second-story windows of the house. A bullet thudded into the tree, a foot from Donald's head. He ducked back instinctively.

He knew it was doubtful if anything would be decided as long as it was dark. But when daylight came, it was going to be different.

Daylight would give an advantage to the men outside the house. In daylight they could either flush the Dymonds out, or they could fill the house so full of lead that nothing could survive.

XIX

By the time Gatewood reached the Majors place, the firing had dwindled to spasmodic sniping from the cover around the house. Each gun flash drew answering shots from the second-story windows and each gun flash from the house brought shots from the men surrounding it.

Gatewood rode down the lane, calling out while he was still a hundred yards from the house: "Donald! It's Gatewood! Where are you?"

Donald answered him and he dismounted, afterward hurrying on foot toward the sound of Donald Majors's voice. He found Donald behind a big cottonwood tree. Len Peabody was with him.

Donald said: "So you got out."

"No thanks to you."

"Now what?"

"Call off your men. Lena Dymond is in that house. If she should get hit. . . ."

Donald said: "Sheriff, that's our home. It has been taken over by trespassers, who incidentally are also murderers. We have no intention of letting them get away with it."

"They won't get away with it."

"I'd like to remind you, Sheriff, that you had Guy Dymond in your jail. His sons broke him out. Then they locked you in. We happen to think it's time all this lawlessness was stopped once and for all. Two members of our family are already dead."

"I'm ordering you to call off your men."

"And I'm refusing you."

Gatewood stared at him. This was a different Donald Majors from the one he knew. There must be a lot of the old man in Donald. It had just taken trouble and responsibility to bring it out.

He knew he couldn't force the Majors brothers and their crew to abandon the house to Guy and his three sons. He also knew he couldn't permit them to continue as they were.

Donald Majors turned to Peabody. "Send some men to that storage shed behind the barn. There are a couple of five-gallon cans of coal oil there."

Gatewood said: "Wait, Peabody." He faced Donald again. "What are you going to do? Burn them out?"

Donald said: "It's only a house. Better to lose the house than a fourth of the ranch."

"You won't lose a fourth of the ranch. They can't benefit from the commission of a crime."

"We're not taking any chances, Sheriff. We can afford to lose the house. We can't afford to let Guy Dymond and his sons stay alive. They killed Pa and they killed Pres. If the three of us were dead, they'd own it all."

Gatewood knew he could stick a gun in Donald's ribs and

take him prisoner. But he also knew it would do no good. The other two brothers would carry on without Donald if necessary. Donald said: "The coal oil, Peabody."

Peabody hurried away. Gatewood stared helplessly after him. In desperation, he said: "Give me half an hour. Tell your men to stop firing for that long. If I haven't got Guy out of there when the time is up, then you won't have lost anything. You can still burn the house."

Donald did not reply.

Gatewood said: "Lena's in there, man. She hasn't done anything. She doesn't deserve to die."

"And what if Guy gets away from you again?"

"He won't because there won't be anybody to break him out. I'll put his three sons in jail with him."

"How the hell do you expect to take Guy and all three of his sons? It's impossible."

"I took him once before, didn't I?"

"But not his sons."

Gatewood said impatiently: "What do you care whether I can do it or not? If I fail, you can burn them out. All you'll have lost is half an hour. But if I succeed, you've saved your house."

Donald still hesitated. Peabody came back, lugging the two five-gallon cans of coal oil. He said: "Now what, Mister Majors?"

"Leave them here. Gatewood is going to try and get in the house. He wants half an hour and I guess we can give him that." He turned to Gatewood. "All right, Sheriff. Go ahead."

Gatewood stared at him suspiciously, wishing he could see his expression. He could not. It was too dark. He moved away, troubled because Donald had agreed so easily.

He had to admit that the Majors brothers were a hundred percent in the right. No jury in the country would convict them for killing Guy and his three sons tonight. This was a never-to-be-repeated opportunity for them to be rid of Guy and his sons for good. He could not understand Donald's agreeing to give up that opportunity so readily.

But he hadn't time to worry about it. Half an hour wasn't much time. He moved cautiously toward the house, staying in shadow when he could.

At the edge of the lawn he paused. Most of the circulation had by now returned to his ankles and his wrists. He set himself, then broke from the shadows and sprinted for the porch.

Instantly two rifles in the upper window of the house opened up. Half a dozen bullets thudded into the dirt behind him as he ran. He reached the porch and flung himself flat on it, rolling across it and against the wall. Someone might be on the lower floor, guarding the windows and the doors.

The echoes of the shots died away, but his ears still rang. Now there was only silence. He heard no footfall in the house. The shots from the upstairs windows had not been answered by the men outside.

Slowly Gatewood's breathing quieted, but for a moment he didn't move. He knew how slight were his chances of getting Lena safely out. Guy and his sons were desperate and heavily armed and they'd kill him on sight.

Suddenly and unexpectedly he smelled coal oil. Listening, he thought he could hear it gurgling out of one of the cans. The can banged against something not a dozen yards away.

He understood why Donald had agreed to give him the half hour he'd asked for. Donald had let him create a diversion by rushing the house so recklessly. While those in the upstairs windows had been shooting at him, Peabody and someone else had managed to reach the house with the coal-oil cans. Now they were dumping it on the walls. When the half hour was up, it would only take one match and the house would go up like a torch.

He cursed Donald helplessly, then got cautiously to his feet.

Even if it wasn't locked, someone was sure to be just inside the front door, so he couldn't go in that way. Without the advantage of surprise, he wouldn't have a chance.

Stepping carefully, he tiptoed along the wall to the porch rail. There were vines and bushes here and they rustled as he pushed his way through them. But he drew no gunshots from inside the house.

He moved along the wall. He tripped over something suddenly, and fell. For an instant he froze right where he was.

The thing that had tripped him was an inclined, outside cellar door. Staying low, he groped around until he found the side that opened first. He raised the door carefully, wincing as the hinges squeaked. He half wished he had told Donald to have his men keep firing. The noise would have covered any he was bound to make entering the house.

Inch by inch he eased it up, and it squeaked every inch of the way. But at last he had it open enough to permit him to slip on through. Groping with his feet, he found a stairway leading down. He descended, lowering the door over his head as cautiously as he had opened it.

He wondered how much time had already passed. He'd had only thirty minutes to begin with and between five and ten of that must certainly be gone. He wished he had asked for an hour, but he hadn't, and would have to make the best of the time that remained.

He groped for a match, found one, and lit it. He was in the cellar beneath the house. There was a moldy smell, and there were cobwebs in the corners. There were shelves of preserves on one side of the room he was in. There was a stairway straight ahead.

The match burned his fingers. He dropped it and lit another one. Carefully he eased himself up the stairs. There was a door at the head of them and, when he reached it, he dropped the match.

He shifted the shotgun from his left hand to his right. He checked the hammers by feel in the darkness to make sure that they were cocked. Then, carefully, he tried the doorknob. If the damned door was locked, he'd have to go back out and find another way of getting in. He wouldn't dare force it because the noise would bring them on the run.

The knob turned soundlessly enough but the door squeaked as it began to open. Gatewood froze, listening. He could hear nothing, not even a creaking of the floor, and that was suspicious in itself. He wondered if one of them was standing right in front of this door, waiting for him to open it. The thought made a chill run along his spine.

But his time was running out. Almost half of it must be already gone. He thought about those outside walls, soaked with coal oil and just waiting for a match. He pushed the door open, bracing himself for the blast of a gun as he did.

Nothing happened. The door squeaked thunderously and Gatewood went quickly through, pushing it closed behind him until he heard it click.

He was in the house. He was outnumbered, but at least he was in the house. He had a chance.

Upstairs, almost directly over his head, the floor squeaked as someone moved. Gatewood listened intently, now hearing the main floor begin to squeak as someone came toward him from the front of the house.

He was in the pantry, he supposed. There were shelves on two of the walls. The only faint light came from the kitchen, beyond the pantry door. He crossed quickly to it and went through, swinging the shotgun muzzle toward the approaching footsteps as he did.

Desperately he wished he had questioned Donald about the

layout of the house. Now it was too late. The kitchen door swung open and a man stood silhouetted there, gun in hand, peering into the darkness.

Gatewood whispered: "Just stoop over and lay your gun carefully on the floor. I've got a ten-gauge here and I can cut you in two with it."

For an instant the figure didn't move, but when it moved, it moved swiftly, swinging the gun toward the sound of Gatewood's voice, firing instantaneously.

The muzzle flash momentarily blinded Gatewood. The slug buried itself harmlessly in the wall three feet away from him. The figure leaped back immediately after firing, and the door banged shut. A second bullet ripped through the door, showering Gatewood with splinters torn from it.

Gatewood didn't want to shoot, but he knew he was stopped if he couldn't get through that door. He'd have no chance of doing what he had come to do. He fired instantly, straight at the closed door, knowing the man was still there on the other side of it.

The roar of the gun was terrifying in this enclosed space. Powder smoke belched from the muzzle, rolled across the room, struck the shattered door, billowed up to the ceiling, and spread back across the room again.

Gatewood went through the door running, striking it with his body and flinging it open violently. Once through, he leaped to one side, put his back to the wall, the shotgun ready, his finger on the second trigger almost tightly enough to fire it.

Whoever had been in the doorway now lay motionlessly on the floor just beyond the door. Gatewood could imagine the destruction the gun had done at this close range. He was glad he didn't have to look at it.

From upstairs, he heard Guy Dymond's voice: "Ross? What's goin' on down there?"

Gatewood did not reply. He tried to quiet his breathing and wished he knew exactly where the stairway was.

Once more Guy called: "Ross?"

Gatewood considered trying to imitate Ross's voice, but immediately discarded the idea. He'd never bring it off, and, if he didn't answer, they'd probably think both Ross and the intruder, whoever he was, were dead. One of them would come down to investigate.

The only trouble was, time was racing swiftly by. And Gatewood knew that the instant the half hour was up, Donald Majors would put a match to the oil-soaked walls of the Majors house.

XX

Unexpectedly now from the head of the stairs, Guy Dymond roared: "Ross! God dammit, answer me!"

Gatewood tried to quiet his breathing. He still had one load in the shotgun. He wished that he had two, but he didn't dare break the gun now and insert another shell. It would make a click, audible to Guy standing at the head of the stairs.

For what seemed an eternity, there was only silence in the house. Gatewood wondered where Lena was. He knew he had killed Ross. No one could have survived that shotgun blast at such close range. She would probably hate him for killing her brother, but he didn't see how he could have avoided it.

Five minutes must have passed since he'd shot Ross. The time remaining from the allotted half hour must be almost gone. There couldn't be more than ten minutes of it left. There probably were less than five. And he still had to overcome or capture Guy and Clem and Nate.

Guy apparently wasn't going to send one of the others down. His footsteps retreated along the hall and Gatewood heard him say: "Whoever he is, he must've got Ross. Nate, you go to the head of the stairs. If you hear anything, blast away."

Gatewood broke silence and yelled: "Guy? It's Gatewood."

"What'd you do to Ross?"

"I think he's dead."

"You son-of-a-bitch!"

Gatewood yelled: "You'll all be dead if you don't give up! The outside walls of the house are soaked with coal oil! They're going to be touched off in about five minutes!"

"You go to hell! We got a right here! Lena owns a fourth of it!"

"No she don't! No court in the country would give it to her!"

"Why not, for Christ's sake? I checked Galt's will with McCurtin."

"Because Galt was murdered by a member of your family. Because Pres was murdered by another. The law won't let anybody profit from murder. You ought to know that."

"It wasn't murder, damn it! It was self-defense!"

"If that's true, then you've got nothing to worry about. If a quarter of this belongs to Lena, then she can get it legally, through the courts."

"To hell with you! Once they get us out of here, the Majors bunch won't give us anything!"

"If you don't get out, you'll burn to death. Donald's going to burn the house to get you out of it." Gatewood realized that if he didn't get them out, and soon, he was going to burn along with them. He didn't doubt for a minute that Donald Majors would do what he'd said he would. The drenching of the house with coal oil had convinced him of that.

The thought of Lena, helpless, being used as a pawn by her father and brothers, and her burning, when the house caught fire, infuriated him. And suddenly he'd had enough. Of Guy Dymond's murderous greed, of the man's unreasoning hate, of his own inability to keep the peace in the face of this growing feud. He broke the shotgun, caught the live shell, and let the spent one drop to the floor. He got another live one out of his pocket and reloaded both barrels of the gun. He snapped it shut.

He knew he was a damned fool but he also knew that now there was only one way of doing this. He charged across the room and took the stairway three steps at a time. A gun blasted down the hall, but the bullet missed. He reached the head of the stairs, diving to one side as the gun blasted again.

This one struck his leg, burning like a red-hot iron. He scrambled forward on hands and knees, afraid to fire because he didn't know where Lena was.

A man came hurtling out of one of the front bedrooms, fell over him, and crashed against the opposite wall. Gatewood clawed toward him, swinging at him with the shotgun as he tried to rise. The gun barrels missed the man's head, striking him on the collar bone instead. He howled with pain and Gatewood struck again, this time silencing him.

He didn't know how bad he was hurt but he could feel the warmth of blood. Or thought he could. He roared: "Give it up! Give it up before I kill somebody else!"

He could see a dim figure at the end of the hall. He roared: "Drop it! Drop your gun or I'll cut you in two with this scattergun!"

Down at the end of the hall, a gun clattered to the floor. Unseen, in the other front bedroom, Guy Dymond roared: "Damn you, Clem, what'd you do that for?"

Gatewood said in a more normal tone of voice: "Drag Nate downstairs if you want to save his life. Wait for me at the front door but don't go out."

Clem came forward, cowed, shocked by Ross's death. He stooped, got hold of Nate, and dragged him, bumping, down the stairs.

Gatewood plunged forward. He skidded around the corner,

through the door, and into the front bedroom, falling to the floor instantly as he did.

Guy's gun roared, and the lever rattled as he worked another shell into the gun. Gatewood could see Lena, lying on the bed, could see her come to a sitting position preparatory to getting up. He shouted: "Stay down, Lena! Stay down!"

He didn't want to blow Guy apart with the ten-gauge right in front of her, but he couldn't see that he was going to have any choice. He shifted the barrel and tightened his finger on trigger number one.

Guy fired again, this time from the hip. The bullet slammed into Gatewood's shoulder and the shotgun clattered to the floor. He knew with a sinking feeling that he had hesitated a fraction of a second about killing Guy in front of Lena. That small part of a second was now going to cost him his life. The shotgun was too far away to be seized instantly, and besides he doubted if his wounded shoulder would function properly. He tried. He fell to one side, grabbing at the shotgun but knowing he was too late as the lever of Guy's rifle slammed the action open and closed it again, working another cartridge into the firing chamber.

He heard that, and heard the bed creak, and he heard Lena's sudden, frantic but angry cry: "No, Pa! No! Not any more!"

Gatewood felt his hands touch the shotgun and pulled it toward him, turning to face Guy again as he did. But he couldn't use the gun. Not any more. Lena was on her feet, grappling with Guy. Gatewood couldn't do a thing but wait until Guy, with his great strength, flung her away from him. Then he could shoot and then he would, if he blew Guy apart doing it.

Lena was screaming, weeping, but her words were understandable. "How many of us have got to die, Pa? How many to satisfy your hate?"

He flung her away from him. She struck the wall and fell, ut-

144

tering no sound but a helpless moan. Gatewood's shotgun bore directly on Guy's chest now. Both hammers were back, his finger tight against the forward trigger. He didn't know why he waited. For what he had just done to Lena, he hated Guy. But he did wait, waited for Guy's gun, now pointing at the floor, to raise and point itself at him. Then, and only then could he take Guy's life. Only then, in defense of his own.

Guy swung ponderously toward him. The gun started up and Gatewood's finger tightened just a little more.

Unexpectedly Guy's shoulders slumped. Gatewood said harshly: "Drop it! Drop it on the floor!"

The gun clattered to the floor. Gatewood said: "Go down and wait with Nate and Clem at the front door. But don't go out."

Guy stumbled from the room as if he was in a daze. Gatewood dropped his shotgun and crossed the room to where Lena lay. He knelt beside her, slid one arm beneath her body, and lifted her over his shoulder, startled at how light she was. She was weeping but he didn't know whether her weeping was from pain or shock. He hurried from the room and down the stairs. He crowded the Dymonds aside and opened the outside door. From there in the doorway he yelled: "Hey! Donald Peabody! We're coming out!"

Donald Majors voice came back: "No guns! You come out unarmed!"

Gatewood stepped through the doorway. He stepped aside on the porch while Guy and his two sons came out.

The little group crossed the yard. Gatewood laid Lena down carefully, propping her back against a tree. To Peabody he said: "Hitch up your spring wagon and put a featherbed in it."

Peabody sent two of the hands to carry out the order. Gatewood said: "Get the wagon they drove out here and put them in the back of it. Tie their hands and feet."

145

Several more men went to comply with that. While Peabody supervised the tying of Guy's hands and those of his two sons, Gatewood knelt again at Lena's side. His shoulder was bleeding, but it couldn't have been hurt very bad or he couldn't have carried Lena down the stairs at all. He asked: "Did that fall hurt you very much?"

"No. I think I'm all right."

He knew he shouldn't say it, but he had to know. "I'm sorry about Ross. He just didn't give me any choice."

There was silence for a moment. He thought she had stiffened, thought she had turned her face away from him. He knew he was wrong when her hand crept out and found his own. She squeezed his hand briefly and he knew that, despite all that had happened, things between them were going to be all right.

★ ★ ★ ★ ★

Cañon Creek

★ ★ ★ ★ ★

I

From the town of Ute Falls, the land rises steadily for twelve miles, through dry grass and sage, until the air thins with altitude and you begin to notice change in the vegetation. The grass is longer up there and not so dry. The sage grows shorter, while the oak and sarvus trees seem to thrive. Pockets of pale green aspen fill the shady draws, giving shelter from afternoon heat to the summer-brown deer, and every small gulch runs a stream of clear, cold water.

The man was riding upcountry when he spied the cow. She lay across the narrow main stream, damming the water with her body. He dismounted, a tall and thin man, narrow of hip from a life of riding, broad of shoulder from working with rope and iron. To windward of the carcass he squatted, and formed a cigarette from wheat-straw paper and dry flake tobacco.

The cow was big, weighing close to eleven hundred pounds. Her hide was sleek and glossy. Good, hard, grass-fat made her contours smooth and rounded. She lay on her right side, and her brand, a Rafter GH, was plain on her hip. She had been dead less than two days.

There was the intent in Frank Shasta, as he rose, to drag the cow out of the stream, but then he noticed something odd about her. Blood from her mouth made a dark brown stain on the streambank, and behind her foreleg was a large and angry lump like a carbuncle or boil. Shasta grunted. "Hell, her trouble wasn't poison weeds. It's something else."

He scowled at the carcass for a moment, then, shrugging, got down his rope and put a loop over the cow's two hind feet. Drawing it tight, he mounted, dallied the rope, and nudged his horse ahead until the rope grew taut.

The horse looked warily over his shoulder, then set his hoofs and lunged ahead. The rope groaned with strain, and the cow carcass slid slowly out of the water.

Dismounting again, Shasta loosened his loop and flipped it off. He coiled the rope deliberately, conscious of the approach of three other riders, but not looking up until the rough, arrogant voice reached down to stir familiar feelings of anger and resentment in him.

"What the devil you think you're doin', Frank? That's one of mine, ain't it?"

Shasta nodded, spraddle-legged, facing this big and rough-shod voice, trying to down the defiance that rose into his throat. Big Glen Hocking had a way about him, a way that grated on Shasta and always had. Hocking's manner was that of a man who accepted no one on equal terms, whose arrogance placed him head and shoulders above all those with whom he had contact. It was nothing more nor less than thinly veiled contempt.

Shasta said: "She's yours, all right."

"What killed her?" Hocking's tone implied that Shasta was personally responsible. "Was it poison?"

"Never saw poison make 'em bleed from the mouth. Never saw poison put boils under their hides. I dragged her out of the water because I drink that water. Anything else you'd like to know?"

Hocking turned to the man behind him, a mirthless, triumphant grin on his florid face. "Feisty rooster, ain't he? Do you reckon he's still sore because Rose run him off?"

The man snickered. Anger flared in Frank Shasta, showing in

his narrowed eyes, in his tightened jaw. Glen Hocking could always prod a man where it would hurt. Frank said evenly: "I could pull you off that horse and hammer the sneer off your ugly face, but it wouldn't change you. Someday, though, you'll crowd the wrong man, and you'll crowd him too far." Hocking's taunting smile stopped him.

"Are you threatening me, Frank?"

Frank snorted disgustedly, and rose to his saddle. He could hate Glen Hocking, as most of the country did, but he could not hate Hocking's daughter, Rose, for taking her father's side. He rode downcountry, hearing Hocking's jeering laugh and holding his back stiff and straight. It hurt him to think of Rose, to think of the harshness of his last words to her. It hurt him to think that she was lost to him forever.

Helpless anger burned him, took him on past his own neat cabin and toward the town of Ute Falls, for the forgetfulness a man could find in the company of others. The dead cow was gone from his mind, forgotten in the poignant memories that crowded over him. But the cow would be remembered again. Her death would stir this country to a bitter violence that could leave no man untouched. Perhaps it was premonition that put such a feeling of morose sourness in Frank Shasta. Perhaps it was his thinking of Rose, and his longing for her. But as he rode, the hard planes of his face deepened and set in a pattern of bitterness. . . .

The town of Ute Falls lay at the lower end of this long valley where the now sizeable creek flowed into Blue River. Its buildings were of weather-grayed frame, false-fronted and ugly. Along Maple Street, one block off Main, were the residences of the town's business people, and off Main on the other side was the inevitable shack town.

Shasta tied his horse in front of the Blanco Saloon, a sudden odd reluctance in him, a reluctance to go inside. Summer sunlight lay in this drowsy street, warm and enveloping. Tall maples to the east of town waved their leaves gently in the light breeze. Dust rose from a freighter's wagon as it rumbled into town off the Rawlins road. A dog ran yapping beside the freighter's mule teams until it tired of this sport and laid down to loll, tongue wagging, in the warm dust of mid-street.

Shasta saw the lithe, woman-shape of Nell Briscoe on the other side of the street, coming toward him. She caught his eye, smiled, and crossed over through the thick dust. Warmth lay in her eyes, and a flush of pleasure ran across her cheeks.

"Hello, Frank. It's been a long time. What brings you to town today?"

She had this odd effect on Frank—that of making him forget his troubles in the warmth of her liking and approbation. Yet there was in her too much willingness, too little restraint, and it had its way of embarrassing him. She was a tall girl, with honey-colored hair drawn back and gathered in a bun at her neck. Her skin was white and translucent, marred by an occasional, attractive freckle. Her breasts were full, and she thrust them forward proudly as she walked.

He grinned at her. "I get tired every so often of looking at the same four walls. I get tired of my own company."

"Well, come to dinner then. Tonight. Dad's going to that old lodge meeting of his and we'll have the house to ourselves." She blushed, still smiling, and lowered her glance. Frank could feel color rising to his own cheeks, so plain was her implication. But he could scarcely refuse.

He said: "All right. Thanks."

Nell raised blue eyes full of impish mischief to his, smiled again, and turned. She re-crossed the street, conscious of his glance upon her and allowing her hips to sway a bit more than was usual because of this. Frank watched her go, and now wished he could have avoided the invitation. Yet even through his reluctance was excitement as he thought of how warm and how willing could be Nell's kisses. He shook his head impatiently and turned into the saloon.

Along one wall stretched the poker tables, green-topped and vacant at this hour of the day. From the dimly lit rear half of the saloon came the click of billiard balls. Behind the scarred bar, Sam Podall, unshaven and blurry-eyed from partaking of his own wares, chewed a short cigar and nursed a mug of flat beer. Frank moved to the bar and hooked his boot over the brass rail. He murmured: "Beer, Sam, but none of that flat stuff you're drinking. I went to bed last night so I feel good today."

Sam slid a foaming glass down the bar. He said: "If I was in the grocery business, I'd get fat. I just can't seem to stay away from anything I don't have to pay for."

Sam Podall was ugly as sin, but his broken-toothed grin had an engaging quality that made men like him. It was, perhaps, not the grin at all, nor any outward aspect of the man, but his inner kindness and liking for his fellowmen that drew them to him. Frank gulped the beer, its warmth stealing through him, and Sam slid him another.

The batwings opened briefly, and sunlight laid its fleeting pattern across the littered floor. A man stepped to the bar beside Frank, a bare, thin-faced, and sour man. Sam Podall grunted: " 'Mornin', Doc. Beer?"

Eb Lowe nodded, unsmiling. He said, his voice sharp and dry: "Calling me Doc is like accusing you of abstinence. I've been in this damned country for a year and the only time I've been called that was when that high-priced stud horse of Hocking's broke his leg. I fixed that, didn't I? Maybe the horse can't run any more, but he's still breeding Hocking's mares, which was what Glen wanted."

Sam raked foam off a beer glass with a polished stick and slid the glass to Lowe. "A cattleman is an independent cuss. He gets used to treating his own sick stock and it's hard to show him how he can make money by callin' in somebody else."

Lowe, still bitter, raised his voice. "I spent two years learning to be a vet. Now I've spent another learning that you can't make a living at it. Anybody know who's hiring riders?"

Frank Shasta laid a $5 gold piece on the bar. "I do my own riding, and haven't enough to hire help. But you can earn that five by answering a question for me."

Lowe looked at the gold, his eyes plainly evaluating it in terms of groceries and beer. He said: "Fire away. You could have bought any answer in my head for a tenth of that."

"What is it that kills a cow and makes her bleed at the mouth? A big fat cow. What is it that puts boils under her hide?"

A guarded caution came over Eb Lowe. He pushed the $5 back toward Frank, and there seemed to be less regret in him at this action than there should have been. Frank raised puzzled eyes, surprising a look of near elation on the vet's face. Eb said: "That's too fast and hard a question to answer right off. I got to see the cow. Where is she?"

"Hocking's range. She was damming the main flow of Cañon Creek and I dragged her out this morning. You follow the creek up ten, twelve miles and you can't miss her."

"Wolves been at her?"

"Not yet. Guess they ain't found her yet."

Eb Lowe muttered—"I'll get my horse."—and swung away from the bar. A tall, gangling, and awkward man, his haste was ludicrous. The batwings closed behind him. Sam Podall emitted a low whistle. "He left his beer. I'd say Doc knows what killed that cow. I'd say offhand Doc was a little upset."

But Frank Shasta's mind had returned to Glen Hocking, and to his daughter Rose. He nodded absently, fully aware that forgetfulness was not to be easily found. Considering this, he knew at last that he did not want to forget Rose, that he could never forget her even if he wanted to. Depression returned to weight his thoughts, and this day, which was to have given him a measure of forgetfulness, stretched endlessly ahead of him.

II

Eb Lowe, walking swiftly, reached the tar-paper shack in a couple of minutes. Behind the sagging, one-room building was a small corral, built of odds and ends of scrap lumber that housed a single horse. Eb saddled swiftly, with shaking fingers, and mounting, headed out of town and up Cañon Creek at a gallop.

Now that his plan was reaching fruition, its very daring began to frighten him and for a few short minutes he considered turning his horse and riding forever out of this country. Then stubbornly he shook his head, muttering: "I'm hanged if I will. They'll pay me a living in this country before I leave it. They'll be begging me to help them."

Half a dozen times before had he made this ride, in early morning before dawn pushed its first gray down the slopes of the divide to the east. The first few inoculations had been unsuccessful, as Eb Lowe had feared they might be. He did not have at his disposal the means actually to infect an animal with anthrax, only the vaccine to cure it, and all of the inoculations had been made with this vaccine that sometimes, and apparently had in this case, actually caused the disease.

Now, Eb felt like a man who has unleashed a monster that might, if not fought desperately and endlessly, destroy the country and the man who had unleashed it.

For anthrax is one of the most terrible and feared of livestock diseases. It spreads in a myriad of ways, by wolves and coyotes that eat the flesh of the infected animals, by streams used to irrigate, by hay irrigated from these streams, by flies. Most horrible of all is the fact that it will maintain itself in soil for years, infecting every animal that eats of grass from the infected soil.

In a couple of hourse, riding steadily, Eb Lowe reached the spot where Frank Shasta had dragged the cow from the stream earlier that day. As he rode up, a coyote slunk snarling away from the carcass. Eb snatched his rifle from the boot, snapped a shot at the mangy and shedding animal. The coyote yelped and streaked into the brush.

Eb dismounted, though he would not have needed to, and walked around the bloating carcass, noting the swelling on the cow's side, the dried blood in her mouth. He noted, too, the abrasions Shasta's rope had made on her hind hoofs, and the tracks of Hocking and his two riders on the ground.

Paler, his hands shaking, he mounted again and set out at a steady lope along the plain tracks left by Hocking in the soft ground. They led upcountry, and took Eb Lowe eventually, by a circuitous route, into Hocking's ranch yard.

This place was different than most of the ranches along Cañon Creek. The log ranch house spread out, a full hundred feet wide, and a porch ran along its width in front. Climbing up trellises to right and left of the porch steps were scarlet roses, blooming in profusion. A girl stood on the ground beside the steps, and, as Eb watched, she plucked a rose, held it to her nose for a moment, then pinned it in her hair.

She turned at Eb's approach, a small and dark-haired girl, perhaps too still of face this bright summer day. Her eyes were dark and sparkling and the rose was a splash of exotic color against her hair. She wore a dress of blue-checked gingham that molded itself to her tiny waist and full breasts and exposed her white throat and the golden locket that hung there.

Eb cleared his throat. " 'Morning, ma'am. Your pa to home?"

"I think he is. He rode in a while ago. I expect he's down at the corrals somewhere."

Eb stared at her, her beauty stirring longings in his dry and crackling soul until she dropped her glance in embarrassment. Then he turned his horse and rode slowly toward the monstrous barn and the spreading corral beside it.

Glen Hocking, big and fair-haired, and another man, he found hanging a new gate. Hocking's florid face streamed with sweat, and exertion made the veins of his face stand out in sharp relief. Hocking was holding up the end of the gate while the other tried vainly to lower the opposite end onto both hinge pins at once.

Hocking snapped impatiently: "Doc, get down an' grab aholt of the end of that gate. Help him put it on the pins. The blame' fool's been tryin' for ten minutes to git 'em both in place at once, an' I'm gittin' tired of holdin' this end up."

Eb slid off his horse and steadied the gate while Hocking's rider lowered it onto the hinge pins. Hocking swung the gate shut, grunting his satisfaction at the way it hung. Then, mopping his face with a blue bandanna, he turned to face Eb Lowe.

"What brings you clear up here, Doc?"

Eb cleared his throat, which now felt horribly dry. He said: "Mister Hocking, you got a case of anthrax in your herd."

"Anthrax? What the devil's anthrax?"

This was something Eb Lowe had not considered, this utter ignorance of the disease and of its dangers. He felt momentarily at a loss. "You never heard of it? Hell, man, it's the worst thing that can hit a country. If something isn't done, it'll sweep through your herd like a prairie fire."

Hocking snorted: "Poppycock! What you doin', Doc, tryin' to drum up some business?"

Eb Lowe swallowed. Anger began to build in him and his face turned red. He said with less judgment and control than he should have used: "You brainless fool, I'll tell you what anthrax is. It gets in water and every critter that drinks the water dies. It gets on the ground and every animal that eats the grass dies.

There's a coyote been eating on that carcass down there, and everywhere that coyote goes, he takes the disease with him. I took a shot at him, but I only creased him."

Some of the unbelieving humor went out of Hocking's face, but doubt still lingered there. "What's a man supposed to do about it?"

"Burn or bury the carcass first of all. Vaccinate the rest of your animals."

Hocking stared at him for a moment, then his beefy face broke into an unpleasant grin. Eb Lowe shifted his feet uneasily under the big man's steady scrutiny. Finally Glen Hocking began to laugh. His laugh rolled across the yard, raucous and mocking, and startled a bunch of chickens into a loud, cackling run. He roared: "Git out of here, you scrawny, dried up imitation of a man. You think I'll fall for a story like that? You've starved to death tryin' to sell this country the idea of lettin' you treat their sick stock. Because I was chump enough to let you splint that stallion's leg, you think you can shove a scheme like this down my throat. It won't work. It won't work at all, Doc."

A sick and empty feeling seeped into Eb Lowe's stomach. He swallowed his choked pride and stood his ground. "I tell you you'll lose every animal you've got!" he screamed. "Every blamed stockman in the country will lose his herd. If the thing gets started, it'll be ten years before a cow can live in this country."

Hocking's face turned redder. "Fork your horse, damn you. Git off my land an' don't come back. My cattle are my business, an' I'm the one that'll tend to 'em. Now move!"

Eb Lowe swung a leg over his saddle. A new thought occurred to him. "Maybe the cowmen downstream from you will have something to say about this. Maybe they won't like a disease as awful as anthrax coming down Cañon Creek from your rotten herd. Anthrax can kill a man, too. Did you know that?"

Hunching his shoulders like a bull, Hocking moved toward Eb. Menace lay behind his glittering eyes. Eb dug spurs into his startled horse's ribs and thundered from the yard, tossing only a passing glance at the startled Rose. Eb Lowe alone could not kill the monster he had loosened. He had to have help. Now that help was denied him unless. . . . He thought of Frank Shasta, who had found the carcass, who had offered the gold piece for information this morning. His horse was tired, but still Eb Lowe crowded him down the trail. Anthrax moved fast. Eb Lowe had to move faster.

III

Frank Shasta pushed open the door of Halliday's feed store, and came out onto the boardwalk. He stood for a moment, squinting against the glare of midafternoon. At the edge of the walk, he built a cigarette and inclined his head as he cupped a match and held the flame against its end.

He saw the awkward shape of Eb Lowe as the man rode into town, elbows flapping with the horse's trotting motion. Eb came straight up the street, his horse flecked with foam and soaked with sweat. Curiosity held Frank motionless, waiting.

Eb hauled his mount to a halt before Frank, and the animal slumped into a dead tired and hipshot stance. Eb, not dismounting, said hoarsely: "I'll take that fiver now and the beer's on me."

Frank smiled, shrugging slightly, and fished in his pocket. "What killed her?"

"Anthrax."

"What's that?"

"Oh, Lord. You don't know, either?"

" 'Fraid not. Should I?"

"You will. You live downstream from Hocking. That cow was in the water. Your cattle can catch the disease by drinking from Cañon Creek."

Alarm stirred in Frank Shasta. "What's Hocking say about it?"

"He ran me off. Said I was trying to drum up business"

The knot of inevitable loafers on the bench before the feed store stirred and gave their wandering attention to this conversation. One of them rose, Jake Halldorson, and the oldster ambled up beside Frank Shasta. Jake rolled the cud of plug tobacco from one cheek to the other, spat, then tugged at the ends of his drooping mustache to dry them. He croaked: "Ain't but one way to cure cattle of anthrax. You got to slit their briskets an' tie a bit of rope in the hole you've made. Keeps the pizen drainin' out."

Eb Lowe snorted disgustedly.

"You're thinking of blackleg, Jake. Besides, that's an old wives' tale and won't work at all. They've got vaccines now."

Frank Shasta, thinking that the news of this disease would travel the country like a grass fire, said shortly: "I'll take that beer now, Eb." Impatient anger ran through him. Crossing the street, he muttered to Eb: "Now that Jake's got the story, how long do you think it'll be before every damned cowman in the country knows it?"

"It'll be a good thing if they do. Something's got to be done fast or there won't be a beef critter left. Hocking won't vaccinate. Said I was trying to drum up business."

"You got the stuff to vaccinate with?"

"Sure I've got it." Eb would have said more, but some odd thought stopped him. He ducked his head and scurried toward the saloon, and, puzzling at this abrupt change in the man, Frank followed.

Inside, twisting his beer glass reflectively on the bar, Shasta asked: "What would it cost a man to vaccinate?"

This descent to the practical seemed to confuse Eb Lowe momentarily. He calculated for a moment and finally said: "If 'twas a man's whole herd, I'd say fifty cents a head."

Shasta drank his beer. Some peculiarity about this whole business troubled him and made him say: "I'll think on it. Let you know first thing in the morning."

He turned to go, tall and lanky, but with an odd and feline grace to his movements. Eb Lowe touched his elbow with a restraining hand. "There's more to it than vaccination. Carcasses have to be buried or burned. Once in a while the vaccine will give an animal the disease instead of protecting him from it. Every hour that cow of Hocking's lays up there, the danger gets worse."

Frank said—"I can't deal with Hocking."—and pulled away from Eb and went out the door. Once more his thoughts went to Rose, and turned bitter. Such a small thing it had been, that brought on the quarrel—an argument with Hocking over that brindle heifer and the brand she wore. Clipping the heifer's hair would have settled the argument once and for all, but Hocking had been characteristically arrogant. "You'll clip no heifer of mine, hang you! I've suspected for a long time that you was brandin' calves with your brand when their mothers wore mine."

He was referring to the time, half a dozen years past, when, in honest error, Frank had misbranded a calf. Shasta had said patiently, but with his anger choking him: "I vented my brand on that one, and put yours on."

"After you got caught. But how many times have you got away with it?"

Frank had hit him then. Pounded and hammered and beat him back until the gun barrel of one of Hocking's rider's stopped him. Hocking had forbidden him to see Rose, had forbidden her to see Frank. And Rose, torn between Hocking and Frank, had chosen to stay loyal to her father.

Afternoon wore itself away into early evening, and the sun dropped behind the cedar hills to the west of town, flaming briefly, then bowing to the drifting soft gray that settled over the country like a down comforter. Knots of men stood before the hotel and the saloon, and their talk, while soft, was full of concern and could presage nothing but trouble. It was the talk of men who are slow to rouse, slow to anger. But along with this talk was a rising panic that showed now only in their eyes, in the nervous gestures of their hands.

Walking toward the square, two-storied house where Nell Briscoe lived with her father, Frank Shasta caught snatches of this talk.

"I'm irrigatin' out of Cañon Creek right now. If what Doc says is true, I'm pollutin' every danged spear of hay I expect to put up."

"Doc is comin' up t'morrow to vaccinate my bunch. But he ain't goin' t' be able t' git 'em all at once."

"Hell, Hocking's the one that's got the danged disease. If he won't vaccinate an' bury his dead stock, we'd ought to make him do it."

Drawn by the news, more men drifted into town. Lamps winked in the dim recesses of the stores along Main. A yell drifted down the street from the Blanco, and, turning his head, Frank Shasta saw the dim shapes of two men, fighting in front of the saloon. The knots of talking men broke up, moving toward the commotion. Frank shrugged as he climbed the steps onto Nell's porch.

Vague uneasiness troubled him, as though he sensed that this talk was only preliminary, leading slowly but inevitably to the flare-up of violence that could not but follow it.

He knocked and Nell Briscoe, flushed from the stove's heat, and wearing a bright yellow apron, came to the door, smiling and suddenly shy. "Come in, Frank. I've steaks cooking, and rolls in the oven." She stepped back as he entered, but not enough and his entrance put him close to her. He could see the quickened rise and fall of her breasts, the flush of anticipation that rose to her cheeks. He caught her to him, roughly and hungrily, and lowered his hard mouth to her eager and parted lips.

Her violence startled him. Soft and warm was her mouth, but it had its quality of urgent possessiveness. Her arm flung about his neck, fingers digging in, and her body arched against him.

He was breathing hard as she drew away. Excitement and plain animal desire was molten lava in his veins. But Nell was smiling again, saying: "*Mmmm.* You do that like you meant it." Turning, she darted toward the kitchen. "My steaks are burning. I'll have them on in a minute."

White linen covered the table. A candle burned softly at either end. The steaks were done the way he liked them, crisp and very brown outside, rare and steaming inside. He ate ravenously, but he kept his eyes on Nell across from him, turned shy now by his scrutiny. For a while he forgot Doc and Hocking and Rose, forgot the cattle and the trouble that was brewing on the street of Ute Falls. When dinner was finished, Nell excused herself, and, when she returned, she was wearing a dress of red silk, tight-fitting and sheer, that showed each delicious curve of her body. She snuggled beside him on the sofa and he slipped a hand about her waist.

It was almost as though the silk was not there. Her body was hot and soft and trembling beneath his hands. With a little moan she turned to him, raising her lips, and her breath hurried in and out, fragrant and eager.

All thought, everything but instinct went out of Frank Shasta. He caught her to him, bruising and fierce, and she seemed to revel in this rough-shod way of his.

She stiffened as steps sounded on the porch, pulled away, and sat up as a voice rushed muffled through the thick-paneled door: "Frank! Frank Shasta, you in there?"

With a muttered curse, Frank rose. He shot an apologetic glance at Nell and surprised a look of utter rage on her face. This look disturbed him, shocked him, and he went to the door scowling.

Outside on the darkened porch stood a man, and farther, below the steps, Frank could see half a dozen more. The man on the porch, recognizable from his rasping loud voice, was Frank's neighbor on the downcreek side, Utah Benson. He said: "We're holdin' a meetin' down to the feed store. We got to get together on this anthrax thing. You comin'?"

Frank muttered: "Be there in five minutes." He watched the shape of Utah Benson and the others retreat into the black night and heard their diminishing, outraged voices. He turned to Nell. "They're getting excited now. They're getting worked up enough to do something."

He could see the determined effort she made for control, but the evidences of her temper were still in her and killed the excitement in him. He murmured—"It was a good dinner, Nell. Damn the interruption anyway."—and tried to smile.

Nell had mastered her temper and now came to him, smiling. She put herself close to him, but, somehow, there was not the thrill in her nearness that there had been before. She spoke softly: "When will I see you, Frank?"

He hedged: "The way things look, I can't tell, Nell. First time I get to town, though, I'll come by." He moved away, and found his hat. Cramming it onto his head, he went out, trying to avoid the appearance of haste. Outside, he grinned wryly to himself and thought: *Now you know how a mouse feels when he ducks into his hole an inch ahead of the cat.*

Halliday's Feed Store was crammed to overflowing with

angry, shouting men. Shasta's entrance was greeted with yells of: "Where you standin' in this, Frank?"

They were considering Frank's tie with Rose and, for a moment, Frank was considering it, too. He could admit to himself, now that the showdown had arrived, that he had never given up hope of a reconciliation with Rose. And he was realizing, in this moment, that if he threw himself in with these neighbors of his against Hocking, Rose would consider his action as vengefulness, and that the dim chance of making up with her would be forever gone.

Yet to stand back was the evasive action of a coward, and Frank could not but admit that these men were entirely justified in their fear of the dread disease. At the far end of the hall a man yelled: "You're for us or you're ag'in' us! Make up your mind. Whatever you do, we're still goin' ahead. Hocking's goin' t' vaccinate, or by all that's holy we'll shoot every damned critter on his range."

Frank returned: "I'm with you. I stand to lose as much as any of you." By his words he knew that he had picked his path and that Rose would be forever something lovely that could have happened to him but never did.

Now the planning began, broken by bickering, by argument, by lack of an effective leader. Finally, shrugging, Frank assumed that rôle, and agreed to head a delegation to Hocking in the morning to attempt to persuade him to co-operate in measures designed to control or stamp out the disease. But there was no hope in him of success, for he knew Hocking's stubborn and arrogant nature, and he knew that the very appearance of pressure would turn Hocking bull-headed. The road up Cañon Creek was long, his cabin would be lonely, and there was no hope in him now that it would ever be anything else.

IV

Cañon Creek made a soft and steady murmur in the still night air as Frank Shasta rode into his yard. Hearing him, the milch cow bellowed plaintively in the corral, and her calf, penned away from her, heard this and bawled. Frank offsaddled his horse and turned him out to pasture. Then, lifting a bucket off a nail on the fence, he squatted and milked out the cow's two front teats, leaving the hind two for the calf. Carrying the half full bucket, he trudged toward the cabin. The calf's hungry grunting and impatient butting were soft and pleasant sounds behind him.

The door was ajar. Frank pushed it open and from long habit put the bucket on the table in darkness without thought or conscious searching. Then he moved across the room and wiped a match alight on the seat of his jeans. He lifted the lamp chimney high enough to touch flame to the wick, then lowered it back into place.

Something turned him now toward the bed, some odd, animal instinct, and he started momentarily, a tall and thin man whose angular face missed ugliness only because of the serenity and gentleness that was in it. He shoved his hat back on his head, took a step toward this girl, and then stopped, hesitating. "Rose. What the devil are you doing here?"

She sat on the edge of his bed, looking small, looking scared. "Frank, what is this disease Dad's cattle have? Is it as serious as the veterinarian claims it is? Will it spread downcreek to you and the others?"

"If it is what Eb Lowe claims it is, it will. Eb seems to be sure enough." Moving with impatient and nervous quickness, he performed the habitual chores of coming home. He slid the lid off the stove, shook down the ashes, shaved a stick of kindling into the box, and lit the fire.

Then he whirled, determination showing through his

hesitancy. "Rose, hang it, did you come down here at this hour of the night to talk to me about anthrax?" His question was blunt, his tone blunter. And this was not what he intended. He wanted to show her all the things he felt when he looked at her; he wanted to tell her how hard it was to stand here in the center of the room, when all he could think of was reaching her, seizing her, holding her in his arms.

She got up, small and delicately made, but with strength in her for all of that. "What will you do? What will the others do if Dad refuses to treat his herd?"

He scowled and countered with a question of his own: "What will you do, Rose? Will you stand by Glen whether he's right or wrong? Do you have to make it a choice between Glen and me? A man does what is right, what he has to do, and I did not build up my herd, nor the others theirs, to see them wiped out by Glen's stubbornness."

Indecision was plain in Rose and her dark eyes grew large and troubled. Frank followed his advantage with necessary cruelty. "Do you think I stole cattle from your father, Rose?"

"I shouldn't have come. I should have stayed away."

"Do you think I could steal from your father and go on seeing you?"

Now the tears came, welling from behind her eyes and spilling over onto her smooth and flushed cheeks. "Frank, stop it. Stop torturing me. Of course I don't think that."

He moved across the room now, and she fitted snugly and warmly in his arms. Her tears flowed unchecked and her arms about him were fierce and frantic. "Frank, what can we do, what can we do?"

His voice was gentle. "We can do what we have to do, and nothing else. Give things time to work themselves out, Rose. In the meantime, do what you can with Glen, because he's wrong this time . . . dead wrong."

"I know it, Frank. He's wrong this time and he was wrong before." The hysteria went slowly out of her and her body ceased to tremble. For a fleeting instant her arms tightened and she pressed herself close to him, but then she dropped her arms and stepped resolutely away. "There is no use in either of us torturing ourselves. Show me where you keep your ham and eggs, Frank, and I'll cook some breakfast."

As though she belonged here, she set about the preparation of breakfast. Frank kept watching her every graceful movement, kept wishing he could hold her here forever. But he held his silence, for he could appreciate her feeling of loyalty to Hocking, could realize that she would never be happy unless she could come to him with her father's approval, or at least his consent.

He sat down across from her, silent because there was no light conversation in him and because the things he was thinking must not be said. Then he watched her ride out upcreek, and raised a hand in reluctant farewell. As he turned back toward his cabin, the peaks to the east silhouetted themselves against the first faint light of dawn.

He went inside then, sat at the table with the dishes Rose had used before him, and drank black, bitter coffee until the loss of last night's sleep was forgotten and until the sun stained the thin clouds overhead a bright, fiery orange. He should have been jubilant over his reconciliation with Rose, but he was not. The old adage—"Red sky in the morning, sailor take warning."—kept running insanely through his mind.

Frank Shasta stood squarely between two fires today, and knew not which way to turn. How could he fight Hocking, knowing it world hurt Rose? Yet how could he turn his back on his neighbors, knowing they were in the right?

There was no solution but trouble, no apparent answer but bloodshed and powder smoke. Glen Hocking was what he was, and he would not change. Neither could there be compromise on the part of the smaller ranchers. The wind promised by the fiery sky would be dwarfed by the storm of human passions that today must unleash.

Eventually, shrugging, Frank Shasta rose, buckled on his Colt .44 and belt, and went out to saddle his horse and to wait for the arrival of those who were to accompany him to Hocking's today. He would do his best, and no man could do more.

With a pan of oats, he caught the gentle, spotted pony he had ridden the day before. On him he roped the bigger, tougher black far out in the pasture. Leading him, he came back, and, as he finished hanging saddles, Utah Benson rode into the yard with four others behind him.

Utah was a short, broad man, whose voice was harsh and rasping, and who had no sense of humor at all. In the strictest sense of the word, he was a good neighbor, but he was no company for a lonely man. Frank rose to his saddle, noting the presence of revolver and belt at each man's waist, the rifles nearly hidden in their saddle boots. Eb Lowe rode at the tail end of the column, elbows flapping, and something akin to cold fear tracing its ugly finger across his sour features.

Shasta said as they left the yard: "We will get nowhere at all with threats, so don't use them." Even as he spoke, he could sense the mental reservation that was in these men at his words.

No compromise was in them, only the panic of epidemic, only cold fear of the loss of everything they had built up over the years.

Utah Benson said stolidly and resolutely: "He will listen to us or we will make him listen. I for one do not intend to have my cattle catch this thing if it can be avoided."

More for the purpose of taking their minds from Hocking than for any other reason, Frank put a question to Lowe: "How do you reckon the disease got started here, Doc? Seems kind of funny."

Eb Lowe, unnecessarily shrill, harked: "What you trying to say, Shasta? Anthrax comes to a country in any of a thousand ways. Don't be suggesting anything."

Frank was taken aback, but, viewing the vet's obvious proddiness, he held his silence. Benson rasped: "What the devil's eatin' you, Doc? Scared?" He laughed loudly and harshly. Eb Lowe stiffened as though to protest, but then he subsided into his saddle, and to Frank it seemed that a secret satisfaction lurked in his bony face. But all he said was: "Maybe I am. Maybe I don't like gun play and fighting."

This way, bickering and nervous on the prod, the six of them passed through the gate in Frank Shasta's fence and came onto Glen Hocking's range. At 8:30 they came to the dead cow and all dismounted to examine her, carefully, from the windward side, for the sweet, cloying odor of decaying flesh was nearly overpowering.

Satisfied, they set about gathering dry wood from the brush thickets nearby and piling it over and around the carcass. From his saddle, Utah took down a gallon can of coal oil with a potato over its spout, and drenched both cow and woodpile with it. When Doc was satisfied with the size of the woodpile they had gathered, he nodded at Benson and Utah tossed a match at the mass.

For an instant the match flame burned alone in the pile. Then, with a mounting roar, the whole thing caught, sending its billowing cloud of black smoke into the overcast sky. There was the strong smell of coal oil in the air, the smell of its oily smoke. There was the odor of wood smoke and of frying flesh.

The fascination of the flames was upon these men, momentarily obscuring their purpose. They watched until the heat drove them back, back to their snorting and nervous horses fifty yards away. Yet even here, Frank could feel the searing heat of the fire.

At 9:30, not a quarter mile from Glen Hocking's ranch house, they found the second carcass.

This was a steer, a yearling, but under the hide of its belly was the same odd lump, and blood had run from its mouth.

Now the obscure fear that rode Eb Lowe showed in the man more strongly, but in the others there was only an increasingly grim quiet. With little talk, they again built their brushy funeral pyre over the steer and drenched it with coal oil. But at this one, they did not pause to watch.

At 11:00 they came into Glen Hocking's yard, and at the same time the wind carried a chill of its high country origin so that it even affected their horses' hides.

Utah Benson, his voice taking authority from Frank, bellowed toward the house: "Hocking!"

The grim knot of ranchers and the terrified veterinarian rode stubbornly toward the house and held their milling horses before the wide steps, before the flaming roses on either side.

Hocking came onto the porch, his face showing knowledge of their purpose, but also showing his will and his unbending stubbornness. He said: "Get out of my yard. Get off my land. The next man that shoves his nose into my business will get something he didn't bargain for."

No blustering. No shouting. Before Benson could frame his reply, Hocking turned back through the door and slammed it behind him.

V

Doc Lowe left the group at the edge of town, turning now toward the tar-paper shack and the ramshackle corral behind it. He turned his horse into the corral, forked down some hay, and trudged wearily toward the house. Depression put a sag to his bony shoulders, for this was not turning out at all as he had planned it.

So far, all he had stirred up was trouble, and with the exception of John Rance, who wanted his ten head vaccinated, no one had mentioned employing Doc to vaccinate. He entered his cabin and headed for the stove, but, as he slid off the lid, his eye caught sight of the mess on the floor. The antiseptic odor of vaccines and medicines filled the room. The door of the wooden cabinet where he kept these things was ajar, but the cabinet was empty. All of Doc's anthrax vaccine made a wet stain on the floor amid the litter of broken bottles. A hammer lay in the center of the mess.

For an instant Eb Lowe stood, silent and still. Then rage seeped slowly into his eyes, turned his face scarlet, made the veins stand out on his forehead. His eyes took on the wild look of madness. Everything Eb Lowe had in the world was invested in those countless tiny vials of vaccine. His future was tied up in them, and the salvation of the Cañon Creek country. Who could—who would be so vicious as to destroy them?

Now, suddenly, flight was the only thought in Eb Lowe's head. With shaking hands, he shaved a stick of kindling onto the floor, piled sticks of wood over it. He touched a match to the pile, snatched what few clothes he had from the untidy pile on the bed, and, tying them into a bundle as he ran, he made his way back out to the corral. He had the sweated and weary horse saddled and was swinging into the saddle when Frank Shasta approached down the alley.

Without preamble, Frank asked: "Doc, how much vaccine have you got? How many cattle can you vaccinate?"

Doc, panic putting a cold chill in his bones, shot a glance toward his shack. Smoke poured already from the open door, but Shasta had his back to the shack and had not yet noticed it.

Eb Lowe had too much guilt, and too much fear in him to

put on a bold front, to play for time in which to escape. His laugh was high and shrill, but it broke and became a babble. He shouted: "I can't vaccinate a single one! You hear that? I can't vaccinate one poddy calf. You know why? Because somebody sneaked in my place this morning while we were gone and broke every bottle I had with a hammer. I'm getting the devil out of this country. What do I owe you, anyway? I've starved and gone without ever since I came here because nobody'd call me in to treat their stock." His hand flung back and came up holding his gun, its muzzle trembling and bearing on Frank.

The wind shifted and put a cloud of smoke from the flaming cabin between the two. Amazement in Frank Shasta's face gave way to rage. His hand shot toward his gun, and it came up, hammer thumbed back. But his eyes were watering and the smoke put a spasm of coughing on him.

Through the smoke he yelled: "Doc, stay where you're at!"

Doc's laugh, mad and without restraint, floated to him, and distance had turned it thin. "Don't try to stop me!"

Frank whirled his horse, put spurs viciously into the animal's ribs. Eb Lowe, coattails flying and elbows flapping, was already halfway up the alley, his horse flinging gobs of mud behind.

Frank snapped a shot toward him, holding the gun high. Doc turned in his saddle, fired twice. One of the bullets tugged at Frank's sleeve, tore his shirt, and brought blood, warm and wet, to his upper arm. The other went wide.

Out on Main stood half a hundred men, grouped before the Blanco. Against its wall slouched Sam Podall, his face watchful and inscrutable. Utah Benson harangued the group from the boardwalk in front of the saloon.

Eb Lowe, forced onto Main by the curving of the alley, burst out before them almost at the instant they turned their heads to search out the source of the shots. They saw Frank pounding along behind Doc, and they saw the column of smoke that the fire at Doc's house had made.

Aroused already, and sensing that something was wrong, they spread out, forming a solid wall of men in the street. Eb Lowe was faced with the choice of turning back toward Frank, or of riding them down. He chose the latter course. He thundered heedlessly at them and they broke and moved aside. Doc's horse plunged through. As he cleared the group on the other side, a volley of shots rang out. His horse hesitated an instant, faltered, and end-over-ended with a sodden crash in the mud of the street, sliding a full fifteen feet on his back before he stopped and lay thrashing, a leg broken.

Doc, flung clear as the horse somersaulted, sailed through the air like a limp and ragged scarecrow doll to land on all fours not ten feet from the horse. Dazed he was, but not out. When he stood up, he had a man on either side, holding roughly to his elbows.

Frank rode up and swung to the ground. Utah Benson's voice was rough and full of violence. "What's he done, Frank?" It was a measure of the respect these men held for Frank, this assumption that, if Frank was chasing a man, the man had done something wrong.

Frank said: "Turn him loose. He can't go anywhere."

Doc Lowe stood, sullen and gasping for the wind that had been pounded out of him by the fall.

Frank said: "Boys, Doc hasn't got any vaccine. Somebody smashed all his bottles this morning. Doc set fire to his shack and was lighting out when I rode up." Suddenly then the thing that had puzzled him and troubled him yesterday was clear in his mind. With eyes narrowed, he asked: "Doc, how come you had enough vaccine to take care of an epidemic, anyway? There's never been a case of anthrax in this country since the whites took it away from the Utes."

Fright and panic and guilt traced their patterns on Eb Lowe's face.

Utah Benson howled: "Why not hang him? He started the thing."

"Maybe not. Let him talk." But there was no conviction in Frank. Slow anger burned in him. The murmur of the crowd was an ugly thing, like the throat growl of a wolf that rumbles in the animal's belly before it rises and becomes a full-fledged snarl.

Utah Benson, his face twisted, cuffed Eb Lowe on the ear, and sent him staggering. He growled: "Talk, or I'll break your arm."

"All right! I will! Damn you all anyway! Sure I started it. I started it and I was going to stop it, but now I can't. It'll wipe you out!" His voice was rising, half mad. "I hope it does. I hope it kills every beef critter in the country, and you with them, Benson. You especially."

His admission held them spellbound for a short moment. Then, as the awfulness of his crime penetrated their consciousness, the murmur swelled and became a roar. Moving with the singleness of purpose of one man, the crowd circled him, overwhelmed him, and dragged him bodily toward the edge of town.

In 1885 they had hanged a horse thief, and in 1887 a killer. Now they hustled Ed Lowe toward the same tree.

They left Frank Shasta standing alone before the Blanco, save for Sam Podall. Sam murmured, clutching Frank's bloody sleeve: "Let them alone, Frank. Don't be a fool."

But in Frank Shasta the feeling of responsibility was strong, for it was he who had uncovered Eb Lowe's crime, and so had brought about this violence. He yanked away from Sam, mounted the black, and spurred the animal recklessly through the mud.

175

He overtook the mob halfway to the aged cottonwood, and crowded through them with little concern for those who might stand in his way. He yelled: "Hold it, Benson! Leave Lowe for the sheriff. You want to hang, too, for leading a lynch mob?"

Hands clutched for Frank, but he kicked them away. He was seeing now, for the first time, that these were not the neighbors he knew. Blood lust had put an unrestrained violence in them that would brook no interference.

More hands clawed at him and at last dragged him from his saddle by their very numbers. Viciously he lashed out with his fists, feeling the solid flesh and bone beneath them and feeling savage satisfaction as he saw the blood his fists drew.

Then a rifle stock smashed against the base of his skull, and he dropped to the ground. They left him there, sprawled in the thin dust, but before they went on, they took the rope from his saddle and looped it about Eb Lowe's neck.

Nell Briscoe, even at this distance, could recognize the shape of Frank Shasta on the ground. Running, filled with terror, and the fear that guilt could bring, she left her second-story vantage point and came down the stairs and out into the street.

There seemed to be a silver mist in her light hair as she ran down the street, clutching her skirts, holding them high.

Behind her, Ron Briscoe's gruff voice called ineffectually: "Nell! Stay here! That's no place for a woman out there!"

Nell did not even hear. Her thoughts were reaping the reward of what she had done this morning, early, while most of the town was yet asleep or riding with Frank Shasta toward Hocking's ranch. Nell had been jubilant over Frank's break with Rose and her father a month past. Yet try as she would, with her softness and her willingness, she had been unable to take Frank Shasta's thoughts altogether away from Rose Hocking.

Today then, early, she had conceived the plan of destroying

Eb Lowe's vaccine, with the thought in her mind that without the vaccine an amicable solution to the difference between Frank Shasta and Hocking would be most unlikely. With Frank forced to fight Hocking wholeheartedly, she knew the chance of a reconciliation between Frank and Rose would become an impossibility.

Almost, last night, had she achieved her purpose with Frank, setting the snare of her physical charms and knowing that, if he succumbed, he would be too honorable to do otherwise than to marry her. Failing in this because of Benson's interruption, and chagrined over it, she had been perhaps too hasty this morning. Now her action was about to cost the life of Doc Lowe.

Flames rose from Eb Lowe's shack, from the corral, and shed to which it had spread. As the roof fell in, a shower of blazing sparks rose on the hot blast of air from the fire, scattering over Ute Falls' shack town.

Nell, past the body of Frank Shasta on the ground, past his strangely staggering mount, screamed at the mob: "Are you going to let the town burn while you hang a man?" Her voice was lost in their vengeful determination, in their hoarse shouting. She tore and clawed her way through their solid ranks and at last some semblance of sanity came to them, seeing a woman here.

She screamed: "Stop this! If you must hang someone, then hang me! I was the one that broke Eb Lowe's bottles of vaccine. If it were not for me, he would be able to stop the epidemic!"

They wavered, and fell back from her, staring at her as though she were mad. Ron Briscoe came through the crowd and caught her arm. "Are ye daft, girl? What are ye talkin' about?"

An odd stillness gripped the mob, broken only by the sobbing, rasping fight for breath as Eb Lowe clawed at the tightened loop of lariat rope about his neck. Into this silence broke the raucous and frantic pealing of the schoolhouse bell, and, while it was yet ringing, the cry—"Fire! Fire!"—broke from a dozen throats.

On the frontier no man ignores this cry. All thought of Eb Lowe was gone, and the cowmen raced for the river, gathering buckets as they went, to form a line between river and the blaze.

Nell Briscoe, pale and trembling, made her slow way back to where Frank Shasta was stirring painfully. As she knelt beside him, she thought: *He will hate me when he finds what I have done. Oh, why did I do it? Why did I do it?*

VI

A thousand hammers pounded inside Frank Shasta's skull, and it seemed as though any second his head would burst, scattering its pieces over all this street.

The softness and sympathy of Nell Briscoe was the first thing to penetrate his consciousness. The second was Eb Lowe nearby, rubbing resentfully at the red welt the rope had made on his neck. Frank sat up. He said ruefully: "I didn't stop them, but something did. What was it?"

"Her." Eb jerked his head to indicate Nell. "She's the one that broke the vaccine bottles."

This was puzzling to Frank, but more puzzling suddenly were the antics of his horse. Like a man lost in the dizziness of alcohol, the animal staggered up the street, weaving from one side of it to the other. In front of the Blanco, the black collapsed, the shock of his falling communicating itself through the ground clear to where Frank sat. Eb was running toward the big gelding, and Frank stood up, swaying momentarily like a tall pine in a gale. The street blurred before his eyes and dizziness nearly overwhelmed him. Rubbing the back of his head carefully, he walked toward the horse and the man bending over it. Eb straightened as he approached, a nameless, awful dread in his deep-set eyes. He fired his glance on Nell Briscoe, his blame and his hate scorching her.

He said in a voice wholly without life: "Anthrax. Look at the lump on his neck. How'd he git it there?"

Frank, confused and without the full use of his wits, stared uncomprehendingly. As though he hated this new thought, as though he would not yet believe it, Eb Lowe croaked: "Your rope. You dragged Hocking's cow out of Cañon Creek with it. Later you roped this horse with it, didn't you?" Giving Frank no time to answer, he screamed: "Didn't you?"

Frank nodded, his eyes staring at the welt on Eb Lowe's neck. Suddenly Nell Briscoe began to laugh. Her laugh pealed hysterically down the length of the empty street. Eb Lowe stepped close and hit her in the mouth with his fist. She stopped laughing and began to cry. Anger stirred in Frank, but died abruptly as Lowe choked. "I'm next. Damn you, I'm next. They used your rope on me. It was so tight it broke the skin. And there's no vaccine left. There's no vaccine left!"

As though he could flee from this dread disease, he turned and began to run, a scarecrow of a man, coat flapping in the chill wind. At the edge of town, he tripped and fell. Up again, he ran until he went out of sight into the thick-growing willows at the river's edge. Nell covered her face with her hands, her body shaking silently. Then she, too, ran, toward home, without looking at Frank, without looking back.

Behind him, Frank heard the dry voice of Sam Podall: "Come inside, son. More than anything else right now, you need a drink."

All through the long afternoon the men of the town and the Cañon Creek ranchers fought the blaze that threatened to engulf both Ute Falls' shack town, and the town proper as well. The flames utterly consumed the shack of Eb Lowe, and three that adjoined it. Toward nightfall, with the blaze nearly out, half a dozen men went uptown with team and stone boat, rolled the carcass of Frank Shasta's horse onto the sled, and dragged it up onto the high ground to the north of town where they burned it and Frank's rope with it. Then these same men went to the riverbank, stripped down, and scrubbed with brushes and strong soap, as though this would ward off any infection they might have caught. Feeling relieved, they dressed then and made their way to the Blanco, to the smoky, lamplit room filled with the reeking and sweating bodies of the firefighters.

Utah Benson, broad and smoke-blackened, stood with bottle in hand and back to the bar. He shouted: "Well now boys, it's fish or cut bait! You seen what Frank's rope done. It killed his horse, an' probably killed Doc. If Hocking won't do nothing, if he ain't goin' to help us stamp out the thing, then we'd better get ready to fight, or give up an' move out of the country."

Sam Podall said: "You've got to have more plan than jist fightin'. You boil up there onto Hocking's layout, an' there'll be a few of you won't come back."

Utah looked around him, slyness creeping into his heavy face. Sam said: "If you're lookin' for Frank, he ain't here. He went over to the hotel to sleep off the lump you put on his head."

Utah said: "Hocking won't be lookin' fer trouble at two, three o'clock in the morning, will he? If we was to start now, that's about the time we'd git there."

He heard the low murmur of approval that rose from the packed room. And a new idea was born in his mind. A man, if he was to get big in a settled country like this one, had to see opportunities and seize them as they arose. This was Utah Benson's opportunity. Supposing Hocking were killed in the raid? Suppose further that the action he and the others were to take afterward was successful in stamping out the anthrax outbreak? Would not the gratitude of these men toward him for his decisive action be sufficient to hold them back if he were to grab Hocking's vast and unpatented range?

Utah thought it would. He shouted: "Well, come on then! What the hell are we waitin' for?"

As the group left Ute Falls, thin and drifting wisps of cloud exposed the full moon momentarily. There was still a chill to the air. Thirty strong was this group of raiders, peaceful men turned violent by the threat to their security.

They thundered across the bridge that spanned Blue River and took the long-rising road that wound along the bank of Cañon Creek. Moonlight glinted on the blued steel of their weapons. Their faces were grim, and if there was indecision or doubt in any of them, it was carefully hidden.

But in more than one of them was the wondering thought as they gazed at Utah's solid shape at the head of the column: *What in the merry devil does he intend to do, murder them in their beds?*

Sam Podall, only slightly unsteady from his evening's drinking, watched them go, standing in the lamplight that shone through the dirty windows of the Blanco and laid its soft glow on the street.

The unaccustomed chill of the air put a trembling in his knees and in his jaw and made his teeth chatter slightly, reminding him of his oft-repeated but never kept promise to himself that he would spend no more winters in this high and bleak country.

Jake Halldorson, tall, bony, and craggy of face, came out through the doors to stand beside him. The oldster, swaying from the effects of tonight's score of free drinks, peered nearsightedly into the night and muttered thickly: "Hell to pay tonight."

Sam only grunted: "Go home, Jake." Sam was fighting a battle within himself. Drink had dimmed its urgency, but as the

181

cold air wore away the effects of the alcohol, it became more pressing and more disturbing.

Jake fished in his capacious coat pocket and took out a battered and curve-stemmed pipe. He tamped it full of rough-cut tobacco and thrust it into his mouth. Sam, watching him, murmured: "How in the devil do you hold that in your mouth? If I didn't have no more teeth than you've got, I'm hanged if I wouldn't give up a pipe and smoke cigarettes."

Jake asked: "You goin' to let Frank Shasta sleep up there in the hotel whilst that murderin' bunch jumps on Hocking an' his girl?"

Anger stirred in Sam, perhaps more anger than was justified under the circumstances. "It's none of my damned business, an' none of yours, either." His glance roved up Main, saw the single square of light in Ron Briscoe's two-storied house. His thought was—*Nell's still up.*—and he felt a momentary pity for her. She was a warm and lusty woman and knew what she wanted. He did not blame her because she had been clumsy in her method of going after it.

Trying as much to justify the doubt in his own mind as to justify himself in Jake's eyes, Sam said: "Frank's taken an awful wallop on the head. He's apt to be hazy anyway. If I was to go wake him up, he'd only chase up there an' get himself killed. Would that be doin' him a favor?"

Jake shrugged. "Guess not." Stepping carefully, he crossed the street and disappeared into the dark passageway between the bank and the mercantile store. Sam Podall stood a moment more, then, shrugging, turned back into his now empty saloon. As the doors swung to behind him, he heard a step on the walk. He growled—"No more tonight. I'm closin' up."—and started to swing shut the heavy inner doors. But the voice from outside stopped him, for it was a woman's voice. "Wait."

He whirled. Nell Briscoe, shawl-wrapped and white-faced,

stood on the walk. Fright was in her eyes. She looked as though she were poised for flight. She cried softly: "You've got to wake Frank."

"And let him go up there and get killed?"

She nodded. "If that is the way it has to be."

Sam nodded wearily. "I guess you're right. I've been thinking the same thing myself all evening." He moved into the saloon, blew out the lamps, and returned, closing the doors and locking them behind him. He took her elbow and steered her up Main toward home. He said: "I'll wake him and I'll ride with him."

He was smelling the woman fragrance of her, strongly stirred, and suddenly he wished he were not so ugly, wished he were in some business other than the saloon business.

Nell was sobbing softly as he left her at her door. Moving swiftly, he went down Main and entered the Elkhorn Hotel. A single lamp burned dimly on the desk, and the bespectacled clerk snored lustily behind it. Stepping softly, Sam went past him and climbed the creaking stairs.

He had no trouble finding Frank's room, for he had helped Frank up here this evening himself. Without knocking, he went in and struck a match. Frank Shasta rose on an elbow sleepily, blinking against the flare of the match.

Sam Podall whispered: "Get your boots on, Frank. Utah Benson and thirty others are headin' for Hocking's, an' they're loaded for bear."

VII

The air cleared up here in the high country much sooner than it did lower down in the valley of the Blue. Rose Hocking stood on the long verandah at sundown, smelling the cleanness of the air, the chill fragrance of the spruces that crowded against the back of the big house. Silence lay over the land, except for the small metallic sounds as the crew moved about their last chores preparatory to entering the bunkhouse for supper.

Blue, fragrant cedar smoke drifted from the bunkhouse chimney, rising and, to Rose, forecasting a fair day for tomorrow. Boiling coffee and frying beef spread and mingled their homey fragrances with these other, wilder smells.

Glen Hocking came home from his ride, big and blustering in his wool-plaid coat and stiff, batwing chaps, damp and strong with the smell of man and horse. Climbing the porch steps, he caught Rose beneath her arms and tossed her effortlessly into the air, just as he had when she was a tiny girl. She frowned, displeased with him, and wondering how she could make him see that he could not ride rough-shod over his downcreek neighbors forever without paying for it. Trouble, poorly concealed, rode the creases on Glen Hocking's brow. Rose asked: "Did you find some more?"

"Two. Hang it, I wonder how the thing got started."

"You should have let the vet vaccinate."

He snorted, but conviction was lacking in him. "We burned the two we found. Mind you, I ain't sayin' Doc was right, but burnin' the carcasses sure won't hurt nothin'."

Rose followed him into the house, her earlier assurance melting oddly before his easy arrogance. Yet there was no lessening of her purpose.

With characteristic unconcern for the cleanliness of the house, he stamped his heavy boots before the fireplace and shucked out of his coat, tossing it carelessly on the floor.

Rose, tiny but stiff with determination, said in a still, soft voice: "I will be leaving here tomorrow. When this is over, if he is alive, Frank will come for me and we will be married. If he is not alive, I will never want to see either you or this country again."

There. It was said. Now she waited for the storm to break.

For a moment she thought he had not heard, for he continued

his shrugging and stamping and wheezing, backing himself scorchingly close to the fire as though to soak its welcome warmth clear to his bones. He waited, and he waited, and Rose knew at last that he was digesting her rebellion, was perhaps for the first time in his life thinking out a problem before he began the shouting.

She could not know how much she looked like her mother had looked, standing there, nor that her words of revolt were in very nearly the same tone and voice that her mother had used years before.

Yet she did know this, that no one forced Glen Hocking, for it was ingrained in him that pressure only firmed his stubbornness and stirred his anger.

The small pressure Rose put upon him now had this effect. He said coldly: "If that is the way you want it, then that is the way it will have to be. Do you think that I will crawl or beg or change the things I intend to do because you threaten me?"

"I am not threatening. I have never threatened. But there was threat enough today in Utah Benson and in those with him. It should have made you think. Frightened men are dangerous, Dad. The men with Utah Benson were frightened men. And you have put Frank in the middle. If he sides with them, he must fight you and, indirectly, me."

Her voice rose only slightly, but desperation ran through her words. "I won't put him in that position, Dad. I won't have him feeling that he is betraying me by doing what he thinks is right. And I won't run the risk of having him fight his neighbors because he will not fight you."

Glen Hocking sat down heavily. His voice was coarse and full of hate. He growled: "Get out of my sight."

Rose hesitated, remorseful and feeling tears forming behind her eyes. If she could only explain—make him see—soften him.

He turned his face full toward her, eyes blazing and mouth a bitter, thin line. He shouted: "Damn it, get out of my sight! Can't you hear?"

Rose turned and went out, down the long, dim hallway to her own room. Frustration and anger were strong in her, but there was something else, something that made the flood of tears come, made her body shake with sobs. It was pity. Pity for her father because he could not change, because his own way and his own stubbornness were more important to him than even his own flesh and blood.

Into her valise she packed the clothes she wanted to take, and then she stretched herself out on the bed, appalled at the irrevocability of the step she had taken, but full of relief because she would no longer be forced into conflict with either Frank or with Glen Hocking, both of whom she loved.

Once, at midnight, she wakened from a nightmare of vague and obscure terror, but, hearing nothing, she forced relaxation into her body and did not wake again until Utah Benson rode, howling, into the yard.

Buckling his gun belt as he ran, Frank Shasta took the hotel steps two at a time, and half a dozen steps behind him ran Sam Podall.

As they passed the desk, the clerk roused with a start, but he had no time to speak before Frank and Sam burst through the door and were gone. Down the silent and deserted street toward the long livery barn ran the two, with Sam yelling breathlessly from behind: "I got a couple of pretty good horses in the livery barn."

Frank muttered under his breath: "They'll have to be good." Aloud he asked: "How much start has Utah got?"

"An hour. No more than that. He said somethin' about gettin' to Hocking's about three, four o'clock in the morning. So he's allowing plenty of time an' keepin' his horses fresh."

A precious ten minutes were lost in locating Sam's horses in the pitch-black of the stable, saddling, and leading them outside. Then, sparing neither spur nor quirt, Frank galloped across the bridge and took the winding road up Cañon Creek.

His horse was a big, dappled gray, black of mane and tail, whose eagerness and willingness to run bespoke the heavy ration of grain to which he was accustomed. But Frank pulled him back into a fast, mile-eating trot, for he knew that a fat and grain-fed horse will tire fast and sweat easily.

Ranging up beside him, Sam asked: "What you goin' to do, Frank? There's thirty men with Utah."

"Hell, I don't know. Get there first of all. After that. . . ." It was difficult for him to hold the horse in, but he knew that, if he did not, the animal would play out on him.

The moon settled toward the horizon, and the air turned colder with the clearing skies.

At 1:30, they passed through Frank's place, and at two came onto Hocking's vast domain. Oddly enough, the disturbing thing in Frank Shasta's mind was not the thirty men with Utah Benson, but Benson himself. Nor did he worry now about which side of this fight he must take. That had been decided for him. This raid before dawn had robbed the small ranchers of whatever right might have been on their side. What they planned, what Benson planned, and what they backed him up in, was murder and destruction, not the honest fight of men crowded against a wall.

Sam Podall, as though sensing his thoughts, said: "The way to beat any opposition is to remove the guy in the driver's seat. If you're with the mob, get Hocking. If you're with Hocking, get Benson."

Frank's tone was bitter. "How are you going to do that in a pitch-black yard with thirty or forty men milling around and all of them shooting?" He thought for a moment, saying finally:

"Benson's after something. He's never stood at the head of anything before. Why is he doing it now?"

"What is any man after in a country where there's more cattle than there is grass, where there's more men than there is land? Hocking holds his grass by force. If Hocking was to get killed tonight, who could hold his grass for him?"

Half a mile from Hocking's house, Frank heard the distant popping of the guns, and now he sank spurs into the gray's ribs, forcing him forward, forcing from him every last ounce of power that was left.

VIII

Rose leaped from her bed as the noise of shots racketed across the yard, entering the closed windows of the house. Yells volleyed back and forth between bunkhouse and house, and bullets made a solid, deadened sound as they imbedded themselves in the log walls.

Snatching a woolen robe, she sped barefooted down the hall, bursting into the big front room immediately behind the bullroaring bulk of her father. Alone these two were in the big house, for Glen Hocking would tolerate not even the cook sleeping in the house. Hastily Rose ran to the door and dropped the heavy oak bar into place. Speeding to the rear door, she did the same there. Glass, shattered by bullets, made a continuing, tinkling sound.

Hocking roared as she returned: "This is the work of that jigger you want to marry! You still want to go with him?"

"Frank would have no part in this." She was adamant and white-faced. Now she could hear, from the direction of the bunkhouse, the volley of answering shots that the crew poured into the milling shapes in the yard. Crowded recklessly against a broken window, she heard a harsh yell of pain, saw a man go tumbling to the ground, only a dim shape in the air as he fell, only a shapeless lump on the ground afterward.

Utah Benson's harsh shout was solid and tangible enough in the unearthly tangle of milling horses and running men: "Take cover, damn you! We got all night to smoke 'em out!"

Glen Hocking thrust Rose aside with a rough and peremptory hand, then flung a shot from his six-shooter at the sound of the voice. An answering burst beat out the remaining glass from the window near the fireplace.

Rose called, panic touching her: "Dad, are you hurt?"

His voice was a growl of rage beneath the window sill: "Nicked."

Utah Benson's harsh yell rolled across the yard again, this time directed at Glen Hocking within the house: "Come out with your hands up! You're out of business, because we're goin' to kill every rotten cow in your herd! But there's time to save your life if you come out now!"

For answer, Hocking emptied his Colt into the blurring and melting shapes in the yard, scoring at least one hit on a horse, for the animal screamed and went down kicking.

Silence lay, heavy and menacing, now, broken only by the small sounds of movement, but by no shots. There was the murmur of voices in the timber behind the house, and then suddenly the ring of axes. Benson's words—". . . smoke 'em out!"—suddenly started running through Rose's head repetitiously. She cried: "Oh, Dad, they're going to set fire to the house! Why? Why? You've done nothing to deserve this. You were stubborn and you were wrong, but people don't burn a man's house for being stubborn and wrong."

He said: "You were leaving. Now is the time to do it. Open the door and sing out who you are. Even those stinking rats out there wouldn't shoot a woman." There was no condemnation in his tone, only the gall-bitter hate of an arrogant man brought to earth, and it was directed at the men outside, not at Rose.

189

"You know I won't leave you now." She murmured this almost absently, wondering all the while: *Where is Frank? Oh, where is Frank? Why doesn't he come?* It did not occur to her at all that Frank could be there in the yard. She knew he was incapable of joining such a thing as this. She knew, too, that he was incapable of stopping it. This action tonight was like the thunderous flood that could roar down Cañon Creek after a cloudburst, destroying every living thing in its path and never halting until its fury and violence were spent.

Tiny and pale, she listened to the grunting sounds of the straining men as they dragged dead logs from the timber and piled them against the house. Glen Hocking, raging helplessly, ran from window to window, firing at sounds, at imagined movements, but hitting nothing. Now all firing had ceased at the bunkhouse, for to fire at the raiders meant firing at the house.

Hope was gone from Rose entirely as she waited for the flames to mount, for the intense heat that would inevitably drive both her and her father into the open.

The first tiny flames were licking upward as Frank Shasta and Sam thundered around a bend in the road and into the huge clearing where Hocking's sprawling ranch buildings clustered. Frank's head throbbed mercilessly, and the scene before him was blurred and swimming wildly before his eyes. His first reaction was a terrible and overpowering rage, but the steady hand of Sam on his sleeve had its quieting effect, as did Sam's cautious: "Easy now, Frank. You can't whip the whole bunch of them by yourself."

Deviousness had never been one of Frank's characteristics. His was the direct way, which in part perhaps explained his failure to get along with Glen Hocking. He said: "I can sure as hell try."

"There's a better way. Hocking's got eight or ten men in the bunkhouse that'd take a hand in the fight if they could get out."

Frank heard the ring of axes in the timber behind the house, heard Benson's voice, cursing, directing this work. Leaving their horses, Frank and Sam skirted through the brush at the edge of the yard in front of the house and perhaps three hundred yards from it.

Flames from the coal-oil soaked wood piled against the house suddenly shot into the air, putting a weird and orange glow over all the yard, and throwing the sprawling ranch house into sharp relief against the dark sky.

For a few short moments, guns spat from the bunkhouse at the scurrying figures of the raiders, and three distinct shots came from one front window of the house. Frank grunted: "Look at 'em hunt their holes." He would not voice the cold fear that clamped its tight fingers across his chest, the fear that Rose, somewhere in that house, lay bleeding or dying. He could see now, in the light from the fire, that not a window had been spared, and he could see the ragged holes in the massive door where bullets had sprayed it.

The compulsion, hardly controllable, was on him to run, firing and cursing and raging, directly across the yard toward the concealed and sniping raiders. Yet even Frank's agitated and maddened mind could recognize that this would be sheer suicide.

His movements, as these thoughts went through him, had become less careful, more hurried. Sam Podall's hand clutched him again from behind, and Sam's dry voice cautioned: "I ain't quite ready to cash my chips yet, boy. Take it easy. It'll be half an hour before them in the house is forced out by the fire."

Frank slowed, and his steps fell on the carpet of pine needles soundlessly. He stayed back in the timber far enough so that when he did sight one of the guards that Benson must have left over the bunkhouse, the guard and not Frank would be silhouetted against the light.

Abruptly he stopped. Before him and to his right, not ten yards away, stood a man, alert and gun ready, but directing his attention toward the bunkhouse and expecting no danger from behind.

He whispered at Sam: "Go on a ways. There may be another." Without waiting to see if Sam would comply, he cat-footed closer behind the guard. He knew the man. This guard was Cy Robertson, who had a small spread close to Ute Falls, a wife turning plump, and four little kids, stair-stepping in age from a year to five

Tonight Frank knew that Cy Robertson would kill him, were he to turn, as quickly as he would cut a snake in two with an irrigating shovel. Yet essentially this man was still the same. This fear and this violence had simply unleashed things in him that might not, under other conditions, ever have showed themselves at all.

Half a dozen yards behind the man, Frank's foot encountered a dead branch. It scratched his boot and then snapped. Wasting no motion now, Frank dived in, running and half bent over. He hit Robertson low on the hips as the man turned.

A sharp cry of surprise broke from Cy, and his hands flung out to break his fall. Sprawling over him, Frank saw the gun clutched in his hand and scrabbled ahead, clawing at it. Cy rolled, bringing up his knees instinctively and throwing the strength of his leg muscles against the weight of Frank's body. But he also brought his gun hand forward, as though to strike Frank's head with the gun.

Frank stopped that gun hand, and, as Cy's knees straightened, wrenched the gun from the unready muscles of his adversary's hand. This done, when his momentum halted, he came diving back again and this time the gun barrel rapped hard against Cy's skull.

Frank got up, wary and nervous, crouching just a little as he waited for the rush to come against him. Over to his left he heard sounds of a scuffle, and knew that Sam had come to grips with the other guard.

He owed Sam a hand, but he owed something to Rose, too, even to Glen Hocking. Bending as he ran, he went swiftly across the lit clearing between timber and bunkhouse, coming up, surprisingly, on the dark side of it without drawing fire from the ranchers holed up in the brush beside the burning house.

A window was here on the dark side of the bunkhouse, broken out now, and Frank paused beside it. He called: "Sam and I took care of the guards. Come on out this window, and we'll show Benson some opposition."

"Like hell! You'll slug us one at a time as we come through."

Frank moved in front of the window, where he was silhouetted against the orange glow cast on the fringing timber by the burning house. He said: "I'll come in. If a man of you gets hurt going out, you can do what you want with me."

Pushing into the open window frame on one side with both hands, he tossed both his gun and Cy's through into the bunkhouse. He heard them land on the puncheon floor, but by then he was head and shoulders through the window. Hard hands pushed at him, forcing him back out, and then the crew came through the window one at a time, eight in all. The last handed Frank his guns, saying: "All right. But what do we do now?"

"Circle around through the timber. Give yourselves time to get set, then holler and shoot fast. I'm going after Benson. If I can get him before you open up, we'll have them licked because they won't fight without Benson, and they'll think you're a bunch from town."

He watched them scurry, one by one, into the timber, and, when the last had gone, he ran himself, from scant cover to scant cover, working gradually across the yard toward the now furiously flaming house.

IX

A light breeze eddied upcreek, caught a billowing cloud of smoke, and rolled it over Frank Shasta like a blanket. And not a second too soon for Glen Hocking, shouting triumphantly— "There he is! There's your boy that wouldn't have a part of this!"—poured bullets from his six-gun at the running form in the yard.

Frank felt one of them snatch the hat from his head and, bareheaded, dived for the ground. The smoke covered him then, and he rose, trying to move with its thickest eddies, moving fast and reaching the brush cover where the raiders hid short seconds later.

In his hand was his Colt, hammer thumbed back, ready to return the raiders' fire and to make the price for killing himself high. But, oddly, these men welcomed him with hoarse shouts, and the fleeting thought crossed his mind: *Glen did me a favor, shooting at me. He did himself a favor, too, because now I can get to Benson.*

Returning the gun to its holster, he yelled: "Where's Benson?" He received mostly shrugs for answer, but one of the men, crawling up through the low cover of brush, tossed his head, saying: "Back there. Just left him." There was an odd exhilaration in all these men, and a wild mob savagery. Disdaining to crawl, Frank walked in the direction the crawling man had indicated, and came shortly to a group sheltered behind a high clump of oak brush. Utah Benson, legs spraddled, stood in the center of this group, issuing orders like a general. One by one, the men with him crawled away to carry out his orders, and at last he was alone, triumphant-looking and flushed with success. Frank stepped from the cover of the oak brush.

He said: "Give it up, Benson, if you want to live. There's a posse from town in the timber behind you right now."

Benson whirled, squat and muscular, his broad face shining with sweat. Wildness flared in his eyes, and smoothly, with his turning, his hand shot downward toward the gun thrust into his belt.

Frank watched him with fascination, and a feeling of unreality nearly overwhelmed him. His own gun was holstered, and abruptly the thought crossed his mind: *I don't even know whether it's loaded.*

Trying to remember how many times he had fired, he shot a hand toward its grips, felt the smoothness of the walnut and the weight of the gun as it came up. He was slow. With Frank, a gun was a seldom-used tool.

But Benson's gun cylinder caught for an instant on his belt holster. Twisting, throwing himself aside, he fired the instant the muzzle of the gun cleared his belt. Frank felt the searing burn of the bullet in his thigh, felt himself falling. Then his own gun muzzle belched flame, and Utah halted, poised an instant in his twisted position with surprise staining his thick features.

The gun dangled from his nerveless fingers and then dropped to the ground. The hand that had held the gun clutched at the spreading stain on his shirt front. He grunted between clenched teeth—"Damn you. . . ."—and then life was gone from him. With a solid crash he fell, not slumping and collapsing, but body straight in the direction he had tried to throw himself,

Frank, on the ground, with no control over his injured leg, heard the coming of the raiders and knew, when they found Benson dead, they would murder him where he lay.

Suddenly from the timber fringe to northward came the rapid fire of Hocking's crew, their shouting, and Frank grinned faintly. They were doing this up right, and even to Frank, who knew better, this racket sounded like it could not have been made by less than a half a hundred men.

A raider bellowed—"Benson!"—and came crashing through the tangle of oak brush. Frank lay utterly still, watching. The man stumbled over the body of Utah Benson, fell clumsily, then rose, and turned to stoop and look at Benson closely. There was panic in his widened eyes as he rose. He turned running, bellowing as he ran: "Benson's dead! Where's the horses?"

The Hocking crew, moving in through the timber, kept up their barrage of lead, their lusty and bloodthirsty shouting. Frank got to his feet, bracing himself against a thick and twisted branch of oak brush. Pain came now into his leg, and from the thigh down it was soaked and bright red.

Pete Worden, Hocking's foreman, found him there, swaying and pale as he and the rest of the crew advanced toward the house. He paused for only an instant, saying: "Hold on, Frank. I'll be back in a minute. We've got them runnin', but the boss an' Rose are still in the house."

Unnoticed by either the fleeting raiders or the Hocking crew, a lone and staggering figure detached itself from the screen of timber behind the house. Moving slowly and painfully, this man made his open but wholly unobserved way to the rear wall of the house. He paused there, gasping for breath. His breathing quieted finally, but the madness did not diminish in his wide and staring eyes.

Now he put a leg over a low window sill, seemingly unaware that the glass cut him cruelly, and pulled himself inside. The long rifle he carried wedged itself in the window, and, cursing softly, he pulled it clear.

The room was filled with smoke and he began to cough, bending double, retching finally from the violence of his coughing. When this subsided, he opened the door and rushed through into the inferno of searing flame and smoke in the long living room. He saw dimly through the leaping flame, distorted by heat, the bulky shape of Glen Hocking, the smaller, slighter shape of his daughter.

He heard the girl's scream, heard the dim and persistent shouts of Hocking's crew as they flung open the big front door and dragged the two clear. He flung up his rifle too late, for, as his finger tightened on the trigger, he found he had no target at which to shoot.

Again the fire-poisoned air flooded his lungs, and Eb Lowe went to the floor, racked with coughing and with no will or strength to drag himself either forward or back. His convulsive finger tightened on the rifle's trigger and a single shot blasted.

Outside, Frank heard this shot, thinking: *Some of Glen's ammunition going off.* Using Benson's rifle as a crutch, he hobbled painfully toward the group before the house.

Hocking, unchanged and blaming Frank Shasta for all of this, raised his gun, but Pete Worden, a small and stringy bowlegged man, twisted it viciously from his grasp. He snarled: "You stubborn loco jackass! Who do you think let us out of the bunkhouse? Who do you think killed Utah Benson, an' broke up the raid?"

Hocking cursed, and Worden yelled at him: "I quit! I don't mind workin' for a bull-headed man, but I'm hanged if I'll work for a loco one."

Rose was running toward Frank. Her woolen robe was torn and burned. Her face was black with soot, and her hair singed and tousled. He thought she had never been more beautiful. He tossed away the short rifle he was using for a crutch and leaned on Rose instead until Glen Hocking, sour-faced in unwilling surrender, put his own solid strength beside Frank and helped him toward the bunkhouse.

Anthrax still stalked the range, but after tonight, Frank felt sure, there would be a singleness of purpose along Cañon Creek that would, in time, defeat it. Glen Hocking had made the first hard step toward surrender; the second would be easier. Yes, with the blackened embers of his house a grim reminder, the second should be much easier. . . .

ABOUT THE AUTHOR

Lewis B. Patten wrote more than ninety Western novels in thirty years, and three of them won Spur Awards from the Western Writers of America, and the author received the Golden Saddleman Award. Indeed, this points up the most remarkable aspect of his work: not that there is so much of it, but that so much of it is so fine. Patten was born in Denver, Colorado, and served in the U.S. Navy, 1933–1937. He was educated at the University of Denver during the war years and became an auditor for the Colorado Department of Revenue during the 1940s. It was in this period that he began contributing significantly to Western pulp magazines, fiction that was from the beginning fresh and unique and revealed Patten's lifelong concern with the sociological and psychological affects of group psychology on the frontier. He became a professional writer at the time of his first novel, *Massacre at White River* (1952). The dominant theme in much of his fiction is the notion of justice, and its opposite, injustice. In his first novel it has to do with exploitation of the Ute Indians, but as he matured as a writer he explored this theme with significant and poignant detail in small towns throughout the early West. Crimes, such as rape or lynching, are often at the center of his stories. When the values embodied in these small towns are examined closely, they are found to be wanting. Conformity is always easier than taking a stand. Yet, in Patten's view of the American West, there is usually a man or a woman who refuses to conform. Among his finest titles, always a difficult choice, are surely *Death of a Gunfighter* (1968), *A Death in Indian Wells* (1970), and *The Law at Cottonwood* (1978). No less noteworthy are his previous **Five Star Westerns,** *Tincup in the Storm Country* (1996), *Trail to Vicksburg* (1997), *Death Rides the Denver Stage* (1999), *The Woman at Ox-Yoke* (2000), and *Ride the Red Trail* (2001). His next **Five Star Western** will be *Lone Rider.*